Wild Intensity

Connection of Consciousness

Melissa Wild

Wild Intensity: Connection of Consciousness

Melissa Wild

Copyright © 2024 Melissa Wild

ISBN: 979-8-9877298-1-6

All Rights Reserved.

Melissa Wild is available to speak at your business or conference events on a variety of topics. For booking information, call (585) 813-5548 or email melissawildinsight@gmail.com.

Table of Contents

Table of Contents

Chapter 1:

Introduction

While writing my previous book, *Wild Intuition: An Adventure in Creative Awareness*, my intuition increased as I practiced the techniques I intended to share with you, the readers. The more focused I became on translating the techniques in an easy-to-follow format with applicable examples, the more I developed my intuition. Creative awareness became an adventure as I foresaw more of my future.

As I wrote, I collected all my dreams in notebooks. I happily followed the lyrics on a journey of inspiration. I spent time appreciating nature. Beautiful connections were apparent to me, and a collaborative view of my future was revealed in small glimpses and sometimes in dreams, visions, and events that were so audacious that I wondered how this was even possible. Life in my imagination became vibrant with possibility.

I knew *Wild Intensity* was going to be about a relationship from the moment I decided to write a second book. *Connection of*

Consciousness was the concept that came to me long before I understood what that meant to me.

Glossary of Terms

Throughout this book, I write about dreams, visions, hypnosis, metaphysics, and vibration. My personal definitions as you navigate this book are as follows:

Dreams exclusively refer to occurrences that happen while I am asleep.

Visions occur spontaneously while I am awake.

Hypnosis is a relaxed, focused state that I enter intentionally to access the resources of my unconscious mind and a higher level of knowledge.

Metaphysical refers to anything that occurs beyond physical reality.

Vibration refers to the energetic feelings of expanding beyond the physical body.

All other concepts are intentionally left undefined for the benefit of the reader to generate their own interpretation.

Chapter 2:

The Map

Onto the beach.

Into the desert.

It's illusive like a mirage.

And I wonder, does this place even exist?

Where is it?

It was the prophetic answer to my question, the exact description of where I was actually going to meet the man of my dreams, just as I had asked.

Chapter 3:

My Dreams

The dreams began many years ago. Initially, a man with blond hair and blue eyes would stand in the background staring at me. There was something familiar about his stare as if I had experienced this stare from this man in the past.

This mysterious man repeatedly appeared in the background of my dreams, watching me from a distance. I wondered who he was. I spoke to him in dreams. He heard me talking to him and didn't respond; he just stared at me.

Recurrent Nightmares

He haunted me in recurrent nightmares I had about a relationship. He was always there watching the sequence of the nightmares with me. His eyes and facial expressions communicated his dissatisfaction with the dynamics of the relationship. I felt as if he recognized my feelings of being unheard and unvalued.

The first time he spoke to me was in my nightmares. He persistently wanted me to leave that relationship. I could not understand why he was there or why he cared about what I did. At that time, I wasn't ready to listen to him. Nevertheless, he continued to enter my nightmares. There was no way to predict or prevent his appearance.

Healing Dreams

After that relationship ended, he became a constant figure in the background of my dreams, talking to me and working with me to heal. I appreciated him and all he was doing to help me. Even when I woke up annoyed that I kept dreaming about the relationship that was over, I didn't want to think about it anymore.

I thought maybe he was a spirit guide because he always guided and protected me and gave me hope. I dreamt about this blond man around bad days. His virtuous devotion helped me move on. He reassured me of hope for a better future.

Over time, the dreams intensified, and I dreamt of this man even more frequently. I could see him clearly. He's got style. He is attractive and athletic. He is younger than me. He has virtue, and virtue surrounds him. He's traditional, respectful, well-mannered, and well-groomed. He is sophisticated and intellectual. He's compassionate, committed, deeply engaged with what he cares about, attentive, and resourceful. He is reliable, patient, and persistent. He is focused and accomplishes everything he sets out to do.

This blond man is everywhere, infinite in my consciousness. He surrounds me. He is warm, welcoming, confident, and greatly admires my strength. The blond man stands next to me. He is a strong man. He guides me and protects me. I came to appreciate

him showing up in my dreams and looked forward to his appearances. I contemplated the idea that he could be someone I would meet.

Intuitively, I wrote: "The man of my dreams gives me hope, direction, and faith. He's like my god, guiding me to keep waiting for him while improving my life and being strong solo. Knowing that there is a better way and a relationship of virtue and intellect beyond just sex, an elegance divine in nature with the utmost honor, respect, adoration, and admiration, a true gentleman, a strong companion, and love eternally. He is getting closer. I am getting to know him in my dreams. Have we been together in another lifetime? Is he a spirit guide? A future lover? Could he possibly be all three? Guiding me to him. Where is he? West. When will we meet in this lifetime? The value of waiting."

As the dreams evolved, I dreamt of my next lover and realized that the man in my dreams is my next lover. I could see the details of his appearance: slim, athletic, muscular build, blond hair, blue eyes. I feel 100 percent comfortable with him. He is my best friend, and we talk about everything. He treats me well, and I look forward to being with him. He has also been alone for a long time. This energetic, charismatic man is coming without me looking. His energy is intense and persistent.

He needs gentle, feminine love and support. Nurture him, be supportive, have patience, and develop friendship. A loving aura surrounds me, and I must share healing love with him. Radiant heart light surrounds me and attracts him to me. Virtue is where we meet, and unconditional love is the foundation.

Chapter 4:

Qualities of Our Relationship

I thought about my desire to have the highest-quality relationship. I created a relationship wish list of the qualities of my future relationship and the expectation that it would manifest. I felt absolute clarity in knowing that what I described was on the way to me. It happens when the time is right, and we are both ready.

Our relationship is built upon a solid foundation of beliefs, values, unconditional love, compassion, and joy. We are each other's ultimate lovers. We have a spiritual connection, emotional connection, genuine commitment, friendship, companionship, open communication, loyalty, respect, and honesty. We actively listen to each other, maintain presence, cultivate trust and safety, evoke awareness, and facilitate growth. We establish a structure for harmonious partnership by embracing cohesive, collaborative values. Our relationship consists of intellectually stimulating conversations, quality time together, travel, adventure, fitness, spiritual growth, long-term intimacy, an enduring depth of love, and great sex.

We value and support each other's ambitions and dreams through loving compassion. We are each other's focus, mirroring reciprocal love and equal effort. We openly express and nurture our love verbally, physically, and spiritually. He courts me with the kind of love songs are written about. We feel ecstasy and euphoric feelings of soul connection. We have a love to cherish for the rest of our lives.

Then I dreamt of a relationship with the blond man. I see us together in a compassionate, supportive, loving relationship in the future. We are gentle and nurturing and love each other unconditionally. I felt euphoric happiness from our dynamic in the dream.

I awoke with an inner knowing and a radiant feeling of "I'm ready" amplified throughout my mind, body, and spirit energetically. I felt warm, uplifting, exciting, and hopeful feelings throughout my entire body. Be open to receiving a better way of love and freedom. I am ready to meet my intellectual equal, who thrives with me.

When I choose to follow my intuition, what is meant for me, what is best for me, and what I deserve, I will experience. Authenticity is the way forward. Always be authentic to attract and sustain the highest-quality relationships. Genuine, authentic expressions are essential.

Strong relationships and long-lasting love come from friendship. Allow time and go slow. Take it slow and develop spiritual and emotional connection before any physical intimacy. Share our experience in a nurturing, mutually supportive, positive, and productive way. Bring out the best in each other. It will unfold naturally.

Chapter 5:

Energy Rising

Love is building and blooming from within my soul. Magnify its intensity until love is all that is felt. Send soul love to that strong blond man.

I could feel my energy rising to a higher plane as I went to sleep. It was vivid and colorful. The sky was a dark, blackish sapphire. There were blue, purple, and yellow stars. It was a cosmic atmosphere of weightlessness. I was in the ocean and the sky simultaneously. I felt the weightless feeling of being out of my body in the cosmic atmosphere and the movement flowing through the water. I felt freedom from gravity and movement out of my body.

The blond man joined me in this cosmic atmosphere in a spiritual, out-of-body, sexually synchronized experience. I felt the ease of synchronous collaboration with his energy in a euphoric collaborative dance of creativity. It felt sensual and erotic, expansive, light, and fantastic. Throughout my body, I was awakened with euphoric sensations that continued as if eternally present.

My encounter with the higher levels of creative consciousness was transformative. It filled me with love and joy, activating the energetic intelligence of creation within me. This intimate connection at a higher level was a nurturing, supportive adventure, fostering a complete synchronous connection in blissful creation. The unity of consciousness I experienced was pure bliss.

And this was the moment of anticipation, the moment I knew definitively and with absolute certainty that he was more than a dream. He was someone I would meet.

Chapter 6:

Protector

I wanted to reach him in the way he reaches me in the dreams, and I couldn't. It was as if there were figurative walls between us. The lyrics in my mind spoke about him clearing a mess along the way and defining his path toward me. I could see the path forming with grasses and flowers on both sides of the path and trees in the distance. The message: We both have our issues to sort out before we come together. We will let go of past patterns of hurt and pain, overcome blocks, and have a successful relationship. Letting go is the road to love. Healing is an art at one in virtue and unconditional love. The old destructive has fallen away and will continue to fade out in preparation for him to enter my life magnetically. He will find me. Recognize when we are totally in tune and all in with virtue on all accounts.

I had recurrent nightmares of toxic men trying to force themselves upon me. I felt my resistance as each one attempted to overpower me, and I stayed distant and free of these men.

Amidst the nightmares, I felt a sense of security. Each time these nightmares occurred, the blond man was there as a symbol of protection.

The nightmares, like protective warnings, foretold the emergence of toxic men. After each nightmare, a man would reach out to me in my waking life. These strange men all shared a common trait: their lewd interest in me. I had received messages from men I didn't know, who found me on social media and would comment about my looks and ask if I was interested in a relationship with them. Other randoms would make comments to me while out in public. The most audacious was the man who called my office phone number to invite me to his hotel room.

As I rejected each man, I felt a surge of empowerment and a sense of relief. This empowerment led to positive actions, such as deactivating social media accounts that brought no professional advantage, and thus minimized the point of access for unwanted contact. I felt successful in my ability to maintain freedom in my vibe, a clear sign of my personal growth and empowerment.

Roses are a high vibrational flower. Just as a rose has beautiful flowers, it also has thorns that protect it from unwanted touch. Remain untouchable like the rose. It keeps the mystique alive and attracts the blond man from my dreams, who symbolizes virtue.

In a sleep-wake state, I wrote: "Be loyal to my dreams. Wait for what is best for me. Impending joy and love. He is quietly waiting in the distance. We will meet in a summer climate with the sun in the background. Bright colors and the warmth of summer are up ahead along my path. It will be memorable in a good way. Step into the magical dream life. Trust that my intuition is creating a life that matches my intentions and the desires of my heart and soul. I will have the future man, love, wealth, and success."

Recognize when my dreams come to life.

Chapter 7:

Beach Rainbow

I was enjoying the warm Florida sun, a break from the cold, snowy western New York weather. Walking along the beach, I found a bench and sat there, watching the waves and the sky. The distant horizon was so beautiful. I noticed some dark clouds in the distance. A fast-moving storm was approaching. I decided to remain seated and watch the storm. It began to rain heavily as the storm approached, yet I felt warm and comfortable. My clothes became soaked from the rain, and I remained by the beach through the storm. The storm passed through quickly. And as the storm passed, a rainbow suddenly appeared, illuminating the ocean. A spotlight on a perfect moment. The water leading to the rainbow was also illuminated as if it was a path to access the rainbow.

As I saw the rainbow, questions entered my mind. What is your rainbow? What excites you and indicates, "Yes, this is it"? How will you get there? What's the illuminated path? What's your path of love?

I remained at the beach watching the rainbow. Eventually, the rainbow faded away as the sun brightened. I decided to walk along in contemplation of this beautiful experience when I discovered a small library along the way.

This library contains all the necessary resources to get where you intend to go. What do you find in the library? What resources take you to your rainbow? The path becomes even brighter as you follow it.

You noticed the incoming rainstorm, stayed through the storm, and enjoyed the rainbow. You know, any time there may be stormy weather along the way, you will make it through. You can move along whenever you choose to. You have your own library of resources to navigate the way. All the resources are available to you any time you decide to access them because the library is within you. The far-off horizon is clear now and in focus. What do you see? Paint the colorful image in your mind. Make it personal and memorable. Trust it will happen and be confident as you welcome your future vibrant life.

Chapter 8:

Illuminated Path

As I walked and discovered the library, the answers came to mind. I realized that I didn't need to look at the contents of that library because the library of resources was within my mind. The image of the blond man appeared in my thoughts. With a deep sense of intuition, I knew with absolute certainty that he was my rainbow.

On my way to Florida, a sign caught my eye. It read, "I will find you," and then I saw a blond mannequin that resembled the man I see in my dreams. This mannequin was a physical representation of the man from my dreams, a sign that he's coming into my life soon. He's on his way, advancing closer by the day. As soon as I launch, he's there. I can't wait to meet him.

How will I get there? I am already on the path. Opportunities arrive to do my thing in a place where events are happening. Go there and get noticed.

Having recently published *Wild Intuition*, I looked forward to the opportunity to share my original techniques in several upcoming conference presentations over the next few months. I hoped to inspire others with the techniques that I was passionate about. The techniques show ways to find meaning and creative expression in any place. Listen within for guidance and look among your surroundings for answers.

Let every day become a vacation-like feeling of vibrant energy. Focus on feeling vibrant energy daily and believe in myself. Bring out my vibrant, fiery, bold, action-oriented characteristics with authentic confidence. Continue to be well-dressed in figure-flattering, fashion-forward statement pieces and bodycon dresses, showing off my perfect body. My red hair is long and voluminous. I am magnetic and attractive.

I am well-recognized and well-received, and all eyes will be on me. My calm demeanor draws others in. They all want to meet me. My story resonates in a deeply memorable way. It's a lifestyle, an experience, and a story beyond illusion. Share the adventure in creative awareness. Focus on my passion for creativity and intuition. Give the audience a unique experience. Make them the star of the show. Apply my powerful intellect, intuition, and creative approach to awaken people's collective excitement and illuminate hopes and dreams.

Follow my dream guidance and live authentically.

Chapter 9:

Intuitive Certainty

Once I truly believed and accepted that the man of my dreams was a real person, I knew with intuitive certainty I would meet him at one of the upcoming conferences. The closer it got to the time, the more there were dreams and a sense of heightened attention to each moment of my waking life as if I needed to be ready at any moment. As I followed my intuition, I determined that he was already within one of my networks: creativity or, most likely, hypnosis. Then, I knew I would meet the man I had been dreaming about for years that summer.

As the days drew closer, emotions flowed along with a deep internal knowing. I felt absolute clarity in knowing I was about to meet this man. He's coming into my life now, and I will know it immediately. So, will he. Enjoy it! Be ready for anything. Be my authentic, creative, fiery, attractive, magnetic self. Express myself confidently. I'll make a significant impression. Welcome him into my life with an open heart and open mind.

An unexpected journey within results in transcendence, a turning point in my life. The past is fading, and I am dropping it into blackness with a current focus on a jovial, young, fresh showman, removing negative thoughts and fulfilling my destiny. Completion creates a deep sense of emotional fulfillment, confidence, empowerment, happiness, and success. My wishes will be fulfilled.

When the intention of the intuition is acted upon, the outcome is inevitable. Be ready for the blond man with blue eyes. Be honest and take action for future happiness. Make the most of the time now. Express my creativity. My intuition brings the ideal lover. Give full attention to the conference and the blond, blue-eyed man. Joy, peace, and harmony await.

Chapter 10:

Meeting Imminent

While packing for my trip to Las Vegas, I was deciding between my black and green bikinis. At that moment, I had a strong inner knowing. I just knew I would meet the blond man while wearing my green bikini, so I packed the green bikini.

I boarded the plane to Las Vegas and noticed a 4 on the runway at takeoff. My connecting flight to Las Vegas was at Gate 4, and I saw 4 pigeons flying outside. The number 4 symbolizes the connection of mind, body, and spirit to the structures of the physical world. There will be a strong foundation, balance, and abundance. This was another indication that we were about to meet.

I was presenting at a conference and planned to post my first-ever Facebook Live marketing video from Charlotte airport with a mannequin I discovered there months ago in the background that resembled the man of my dreams. I was going to mention that I was about to meet him, the real-life version of this mannequin. When I found that mannequin, I instantly knew that he was beyond fantasy. He was real. At that moment, I realized his name. Fear overtook me, and I didn't make the video there.

Note to self on the plane: What happens when you push beyond fear: excitement and liberation. I will have abundant wealth in the form of unconditional love and high income from my business. I will meet that man from my dreams who is my ultimate soul lover at the pool while wearing my green bikini. We begin our adventure together now.

I saw Meteor Crater from the air, and I know it will be a great trip. I love the Meteor Crater. Love is and has always been my guidepost. The blond man from my dream appeared in a vision on the plane. He's excited to meet me today and to spend time with me this weekend in Las Vegas to begin our adventure.

Once in Las Vegas, I got on the shuttle wearing my leopard print leggings and a black shirt. A woman got on wearing her leopard print leggings and a black shirt and sat next to me on the shuttle. This is going to be a great trip!

I got off the shuttle and walked into the resort, and there he was. I knew it was him immediately. I recognized him from my dreams. He gave me a smile and a nod, and I smiled back. He continued walking along his way, and I checked in at the conference. From there, and as always when I travel, I go right to the pool.

Chapter 11:

Mirage is Reality

A sudden burst of excitement overtook me as I was stamped with "BEACH" on the back of my hand, and I walked onto the beach and into the desert to enter the pool while wearing the green bikini.

As I entered the pool, I saw him immediately. It was as if the sun had illuminated him, and his appearance was exactly the same as the man in my dreams. I had been waiting for this moment, and I knew this was it—this was him.

He was in a large group and appeared to be the center of attention. It was apparent to me that he was popular. I briefly surveyed the scene as if visiting my lifeguarding days and determining the best way to approach the situation. I recognized someone within the group who was also a writer, and we belonged to the same writing group. I confidently approached the group and talked to the fellow writer, ignoring the blond man for only a moment.

And, at the actual place in time, exactly as I had described it: onto the beach and into the desert, while wearing exactly what I knew I would be wearing: the green bikini, I met the man of my dreams for the first time.

The man of my dreams approached me and introduced himself. His name is exactly what I had realized via the mannequin at Charlotte airport. I was overly excited when we met for real. He is gorgeous, and he knows it! He came across as quite arrogant, confident, and charismatic. It was all smiles for both of us!

He said that he is a hypnotist, and he asked me a bunch of questions which I didn't even know what they were or what answers I gave him. I fumbled over my words and felt uncomfortable, completely lacking in confidence. I felt awkward, inferior, and somewhat out of place. The feeling was strange and quite unusual for me in this setting. I've been a swimmer my entire life, and the water is where I typically feel most comfortable and confident. I was incredibly perplexed, considering all the indicators leading up to this moment.

As quickly as I approached the group, I faded out and swam alone for hours. I was excited to be a presenter at this conference. I thought about my session and what I planned to share with the audience. I had received messages in the conference app from people who planned to attend, and I looked forward to meeting them. People from my writing group and marketing class were attending this conference, and I couldn't wait to meet them in person and spend time with friends. There was a great lineup of sessions, and I looked forward to learning more about hypnosis from the best hypnosis trainers in the world.

Why didn't I stay in the conversation or ask him any questions? This may be how it's meant to begin, with me not being all ultra-dominant from the get-go. All I knew was that I sensed that his ego was what I had encountered, and even though the initial meeting at the pool was awkward, there was more to this story, and I had all weekend to figure it out.

I had to know. I had to follow the clues and find out what's next. I walked past him at the pool party that evening to read his name badge. Once I knew his full name, I looked him up in the conference app. The only detail was that he was also presenting a session at this conference. I decided to attend his session to learn more about him.

I talked to my mom the following morning and told her I had met that man from my dreams at the pool. I remember her saying, "Blond hair, blue eyes."

And I told her, "Yes, but it was weird, and he is also a presenter."

She encouraged me to attend his session because I had nothing to lose. She told me to take his picture and send it to her. I got ready for the day with a mission in mind and a song in my head that I played and danced to. What is the best that could happen?

Chapter 12:

Enter the Dream

I attended his session and listened intently, curious to learn more about him. I had no idea what to expect or what his session was about. He shared some concepts, and then he invited us to go into hypnosis with him as the hypnotist. I welcomed the experience, and as I entered hypnosis, my body felt relaxed, and my mind became more alert, and I immediately entered that dream. Though I was awake and could hear his guidance, I was within the scene of my dream.

It was the exact dream that I repetitively had about him being in the background, talking to me, and helping me to overcome the trauma from a relationship that ended a long time ago. He was supportive and helped me, just like in my dreams. He was always there in my dreams, wanting me to leave that relationship. He wanted to be the only man in my mind. He accomplished that!

Right after his session, I confidently approached him full speed ahead with precision and focus. I had to tell him. Nothing else mattered. I told him that I had been dreaming about him for a long time, thought he was a figment of my imagination or a spirit guide, and that the hypnosis he had just done took me into the dream. It was him in the background of my dreams, helping me. I thanked him. He joked about me being the reason he could not sleep. He hugged me twice, and we took a selfie. He suggested we connect later and told me, "I will find you."

Just Like My Dreams

He found me at the keynote address, and we saw each other and talked randomly throughout the conference. So many sessions were available, and he had chosen many of the same sessions I attended. It seemed as if we had the same focus and hypnotic interests. So much of the time, he stared at me just like in the dreams.

He approached me and suggested we spend the final day in Las Vegas at the pool. I was all in for that idea. As he talked about running from women, I heard a song playing and heard my own version of the words. "He's not running from you."

He stared at me, face reading and telling me about myself. He was accurate. I found myself sharing my deepest thoughts, feelings, and personal stories that I wouldn't usually reveal to anyone. Despite our brief acquaintance, thanks to the dreams, it felt like we had known each other for a lifetime.

Our interactions in reality mirrored those in my dreams, blurring the lines between the two. I joked about him haunting my dreams for years. I told him I knew I would meet him while wearing that green bikini.

He asked me, "Are you serious? Were you dreaming?"

I replied, "Yes, I am serious. I was awake. I was packing my bag and deciding whether to bring my black or green bikini, and I knew I would be wearing the green one when I met you, so I packed that one."

He said, "Wow, how is this even possible? I have to add this to my story."

I told him what I knew. "Our relationship will be reciprocal. You have already helped me resolve my issue. There is something that I will help you with, but I don't know what that is yet because I don't know you that well yet." In my mind, I know it is trust. I didn't tell him that, or that the words surrounding us are virtue and unconditional love.

Instead, I told him about songs popping into my head and providing a theme song or foreshadowing of what's next. I told him the theme song of the conference was "Dynamite" by Taio Cruz. It was in my head, so I played it every morning and danced to it while getting ready. He said he thinks of "Hypnotize" by The Notorious B.I.G. and sang some of the lyrics. At the end of this discussion, we parted ways.

Chapter 13:

Metaphysical Plane

Our meeting marked a significant shift in my life. Time was divided into fractions, signifying a "before" and "after." I could never go back to before the manifestation of the man of my dreams. I was no longer on a quest to meet this man; he had manifested in my life. Belief in my precognitive dreams amplified, and my dreams immediately evolved into the next phase.

Suddenly, the future seemed to burst with vibrant possibilities, as if I was stepping into the most beautiful love story and receiving previews of what was about to unfold in real time. Everything became even more intense, and I began having dreams and visions about our future together.

I fell asleep on the plane home and awoke in a dream to a nostalgic aroma. It was a signal of ancestral communication. I saw the moon on the Sphere in Las Vegas as the plane ascended into the air and entered the sky among the moon and the stars. A fatherly shadow appeared to my left, and my maternal grandfather and paternal great-grandfather appeared as shadows to my right. I felt a peaceful, warm, and loving energy. I received an acknowledgment of the question that I always ask, "What's next?"

My question was answered. I heard the message, and the words were highlighted in my mind. I got out my notebook and wrote the words as they appeared. It was a message that brought me unconditional love. Allow and accept unconditional love. As I allowed and received unconditional love from my ancestors, I cried. They encouraged me to accept and allow the collective, expansive, unconditional love being given to me. They encouraged me to feel more and allow the vast, infinite love. I fell asleep to a symphony of love songs that inspired me to feel my emotions and believe in my dreams becoming reality.

I dreamt of the man of my dreams, who is now someone I know to be an actual person, and I saw and felt as our energy was expanding as our consciousness was merging into one. We evolved into a geometric-like cloud of blue, purple, and pink, extending out of our bodies into a black sapphire sky among yellow stars. We became weightless, light energy. Beginning with an expansive light feeling of my energy lifting and expanding on a higher frequency, we expanded onto another plane. The feeling continued into my mind, and the light energy from above spread throughout my physical body. I felt him, and I felt pure euphoria during this metaphysical, out-of-body, erotically energized experience. The sensations in my physical body were euphoric and congruent with my dream. It was a great dream that awoke me pleasantly.

The messages about the man of my dreams were clear. I heard words about him giving me the love of my life. I am being given the love of my life. Welcome, allow, and accept the unconditional love he brings into my life.

As I woke up from this dream in a state of half-sleep, half-wakefulness, I knew with absolute certainty that I had just met the love of my life. The man of my dreams is the love of my life, and this realization filled me with a deep sense of fulfillment and contentment.

I then had a vision of him sitting next to me as we watched ourselves in the future. We were presenting together on a big open-air stage with white over the top. Our expressions of success, love, and happiness were apparent as we watched. We were happy with this being our most significant event so far. I felt my emotions as we interacted in the vision and watched the audience and the impressive size of the venue. I felt our happiness and sense of accomplishment, and there was more.

As we appeared on stage, he was wearing a suit, and I was wearing a royal blue dress. The dress was well-fitted and figure-flattering, showing off my shape. Royal blue is the color I feel most confident wearing as it complements my fiery red hair.

Our dynamic on stage was of love. He enthusiastically smiled at me, showcasing his feelings. He introduced me as his beautiful wife, Melissa Wild.

Just then, he reached out and held my hand in the audience, heightening my emotions and physiological sensations throughout my body as we watched him introduce me as his wife. The emotional and physiological response was so strong that the excitement carried into my physical body, and I awoke with a clear vision of our future together. I felt a strong sense of love, happiness, and confidence in my awareness of our future, a feeling that still resonates within me.

Beyond Las Vegas

The next day, he texted me, "Melissa, I enjoyed spending time with you."

I responded, and then nothing.

I read through years' worth of my notes, scanning for documentation of the blond man dreams. I wanted to know what else I knew. How long had he been entering my dreams? How did it all begin? How did it evolve? I wanted to share it all with him and tell him everything. Well, tell him every dream, except for this vision I just had where he introduces me as his beautiful wife. Having just met him, I felt it was too soon to reveal that.

The following day, I texted him a summary of my dreams and intuitive notes about him over the years. I told him he first entered my consciousness three years ago. "We will create something together that will bring us both wealth and abundance. We are on the frequency of virtue and unconditional love and vibe higher together."

He told me that virtue is his word.

I responded, "Seriously?! Virtue has always been the word about you."

He explained it in several texts. He liked the wealth and abundance aspects. I shared that we help each other grow personally, too. Virtue meets unconditional love could be interesting.

And then, he ghosted me.

Chapter 14:

Palindromes

Signs came in a variety of ways after our initial meeting. I began seeing many palindromes. There were too many to ignore. Palindromes represent magical protection. We go back and forth across time and dimensions. Magical balance, harmony, reflection, energy alignment, and interconnection of the universe. Maintain equilibrium. Self-awareness. Look within for the unity of opposites. With magnetism, we are drawn to each other by this mystique attraction of opposite polarities. The balance between contrasting energies is an interdependence of masculine and feminine dualities. We have a stabilizing influence on each other. We bring balanced stability and symmetrical harmony to each other evenly in circular good fortune.

Our relationship is surrounded by love, virtue, loyalty, strength, stability, and protection. All support surrounds us from many levels on higher planes. We are a united force of life and abundance that magnetizes and attracts others who aspire to learn to be as we are.

I see the love we radiate, confidence, cosmic euphoria with all eyes on us, and dynamic balance across time and space.

Chapter 15:

Precognitive Intuitive Knowledge

There was so much I just knew and had yet to share. We are both intellectual, receptive, and open to the unknown. We will play a significant role in each other's lives: healing, love, and wealth.

We are connected spiritually. Next, we will connect as friends and then emotionally. Lastly, we will connect sexually when we have a super solid foundation. All else comes first.

This relationship lasts a lifetime and happened in a prior existence. I carried over a knowing, which is why I've had a blond/blue preference since my youth. We were meant to meet now on this same unconditional love and virtue frequency.

I could feel the momentous magnificence of paradise within my mind as I explored what is just ahead. We deepen our bond and magnetic, radiant love on a trip together on the West Coast of somewhere. Several dreams have shown us together at this place. There are seaside cliffs along the shore, old stone dwellings among tall clover grasses, and lavender fields beyond the sand. We walk along a trail from the cliffs toward the coast and past the dwellings to the shore.

The dark blue water is calm, tranquil, and colder. I am wearing my 3mm shorty wetsuit when swimming. Crabs and seagrasses are easily visible under the water. We swim to where the water is slightly deeper. It is a peaceful place. We are the only ones there for a while.

A familiar celebrity joins us. This celebrity has appeared in other dreams of ours and is our friend, even though in real life I have yet to meet him. The first time I dreamt of this celebrity, he introduced me at the beginning of my talk on stage at an outdoor amphitheater in the desert with hot-air balloons in the distance.

At that time, the celebrity made it clear to me that he could introduce me and get the crowd excited to hear from me and that my content must come from me in my own voice right from the beginning. The power of my energy comes out in my voice, words, techniques, and stories about my experiences. The audience was there to hear from me. And as I spoke, I felt the powerful effect continuing to the present time.

Intensity

Everything intensified after we met. I received daily confirmation of my strong intuition and entered a new level of consciousness. I received messages every morning showing me a love story unfolding in my dreams and sharing love songs with me as I woke up. I was being courted on a different plane by someone here on the Earth plane.

We had only just met, and I was experiencing vivid dreams and insights that inspired me to keep showing up. It was fun and exciting. I felt an ongoing feeling of confidence to persevere in the direction of my intuition.

What is Happening?

And yet, I wondered why I was having so many dreams about this man. What's his purpose in my life? When we are together, how will our relationship benefit each other? Our natural algorithm is together. We are the dynamic for ultra success: our collective energy and our story of how we came together. The dreams and manifestations inspire others. The essence is to show up for each other in this life and be together on stage.

Future money: book writing, workshops, conferences, recordings. Intellectual leaders in our area as hypnotists. Collaboration at a higher level. We bring diverse perspectives that make us successful together. We are equal partners, bringing a lot of quality to the relationship. When we unite, we will vibrate higher together. We rise together.

Do I tell him about all this in detail? YES! Keep speaking up. Keep telling him. Keep the communication channels open and free-flowing. Expand, accept, and share the generous gifts that I have been given.

Vibrant expression is a mode of manifesting the internal truth of my dreams and visions. Sharing the dreams and visions with him affirms them and increases the power of their manifestation. The more I share, the more visions I have. Vision and knowledge in advance create reality. We are collaborators in our reality.

The first time I told him what was next for us via text message, I was so scared to tell him more, yet I felt like I wanted to and just had to tell him what I saw happening. Every time I shared more, I wondered if I shared too much, if he thought I was crazy, or if I scared him away, and the more I leaned into my belief that we had a unique connection. So, I kept telling him each time I had new intuitive information to share. The more I shared, the more he came around. It felt like an acknowledgment of our unique connection and a feeling that we both already knew we would be together for the long term.

We will share our lives and travel together in unity with abundance and success. So much love awaits. We are well-balanced and supportive of each other. I see us happy together everywhere, deeply loving each other and loving the lives we share.

Sometimes, I wondered if this was even possible. Is this really going to happen? How is this happening? When I questioned the validity, wondering if it was wishful thinking, the dreams showed me silly things that happened later that day. I dreamt of seeing trees with strange growths, looking at mushrooms, and walking barefoot in the forest. Then, I found those trees on a hike with my son, and his friend pointed out mushrooms as we walked through the forest with our shoes off. The dreams were showing me what would happen next.

The Living Zultar

I dreamt of seeing faces as reflections that changed across child and adult timelines. There was an unspoken uncertainty as they changed. Where they meet and merge, how and when their timelines overlap and are together. A question of whether either could alter their true timeline, and the answer is no. They were meant to meet now as they are and not regress or speed up time. Just be one as they are. I watched more faces change before my eyes as all the facades that could not be maintained vanished. The states were constantly changing and in conflict as the false faces jolted and rapidly changed. Lastly, I saw myself staring at a living version of the Zultar machine. He moved back and forth and communicated a message to me. Live authentically.

Later that day, the dream came true when I saw The Living Zultar, just like in my dream. It was a real man in costume in a decorated cardboard Zultar box. I approached him and played along. I had to know why the dream showed me this in advance.

The Living Zultar asked me my wish.

I said, "I just want to know what's next."

He gave me a card that read: "If you want the rainbow, then you must get through the rain."

I remembered being at the beach in the rain, observing the rainbow that suddenly appeared over the ocean, illuminating the way and all my insight into dressing well and presenting my original content.

There was another precognitive dream within the dream about the llama show. Well-groomed llamas were set up with clean, color-coordinated bedding for the show. I saw those well-groomed llamas at the fair later that day. The handlers were dressed to match the adornments on the llamas. Presentation matters. They were evaluated based on appearance.

Be the brightest star in the room. Shine brightly. All eyes are on you when you look your best. Invite intrigue and captivate the audience.

Chapter 16:

Love Has a Playlist

Music works the same way as dreams, foreshadowing what's next. Music is a channel and an expansion of consciousness. Trust the music.

I frequently wake up with songs on my mind. The songs enter dreams and tarot card readings and pop into my awareness wherever I am and while doing just about anything. The playlist of songs entering my mind expanded since meeting him. The music was manifesting our relationship. I continually heard unfamiliar songs and looked up the lyrics. Unfamiliar songs played on the radio with relevant lyrics. I felt a love story unfolding a little more each day.

I realized that he was intrigued by my fire energy in a sex dream. The vision was provocative, and I questioned if it was wrong to act as a voyeur of the erotically intimate aspects of our relationship. Sensual romantic songs playfully revealed fun times ahead. I felt invigorating confirmation of the preview of what was to come in the natural progression of our relationship. The songs provoked a strong feeling of connection and peaceful anticipation of shared intimacy as our relationship evolves. I felt satisfied rehearsing the sensual, intimate energy exchange and connection to feel and experience each other in peaceful unity and intense physical, emotional, and spiritual intimacy in love.

Songs constantly popped into my mind and my playlist. The music evoked a feeling of encouragement to focus on believing in the potential of this future romance. Just like the dreams, the music inspired me to trust my feelings and drown out the distractors. I listened for the music as guidance and confirmation. I felt like the songs were sent by divine guidance.

I went to sleep thinking I would write about the songs the next day. The next morning, I woke up with a song playing in my mind. The sequence of songs that was generated after I listened to that song piqued my interest. I listened intently to each song, as I heard them telling me a story in the titles. The message was so clear that it gave me chills. The playlist from the morning I decided to write about the songs:

"This I Promise You"	by NYSNC
"Wherever You Will Go"	by The Calling
"You and Me"	by Lifehouse
"More Than Words"	by Extreme
"All My Life"	by K-Ci & JoJo
"Just the Way You Are"	by Bruno Mars
"Marry Me"	by Train

The songs resonated louder and played frequently over the following days, amplifying the message. This is exactly what I hope for and expect to happen. The music is as accurate as the dreams.

A few weeks before these songs, I woke up with a serenade of songs and a vision of us backstage at a familiar venue, preparing to go on stage. I felt anticipation and excitement as I previewed details of a future event in formal wear on a dark stage. I was wearing that black sequin dress I bought a while ago with no particular occasion in mind. Just a sense that someday I would have a place to wear it. The dress accentuates my slim hourglass figure quite well.

Energetically, I watched from the stage as I shared with the audience how they can enter at any point of their timeline to see significant events in their future by observing it from a dissociated perspective or reliving a memory by stepping into their body from an associated perspective. Then, I moved to the back left of the stage and watched as he proposed to me on stage.

"When I Look Into Your Eyes" by FireHouse entered my mind, resonated deeply, and repeated continuously. When we met, he stared into my eyes all weekend. In the dreams over the years, he was always staring into my eyes. In some dreams, his eyes would change from blue to green, and I would see a reflection of my own eyes in his eyes. Looking deeply into the eyes, they become like a mirror reflection. Inner reflection generates unity, a sense of connection that deepens the longer you look, revealing the multi-faceted layers and levels of complete connection.

When I see him looking at me, his eyes communicate his feelings, and I know it is love that he feels for me. His love is a consistent force that will always be there. The love always remains and grows even deeper, a reassuring presence in my life. I felt euphoric contentment and thrilling anticipation, as if this was a glimpse of the exciting future that awaits.

Chapter 17:

Moments of Heightened Emotional Intensity

As I watched the proposal from various points of the stage, our emotions were magnified, highlighting the love and joy in our expressions and interactions. We were looking into each other's eyes intently. He appears confident as he proposes to me. I see an expression of genuine happiness and excitement in a pivotal, defining moment in the excited smile on my face.

We were illuminated in golden light, amplifying the exuberant expression of love, joy, and happiness in our relationship and, in that moment, leading to another level. The light was our uplifting energy, shining brightly and magnetically attracted to each other in our own universe, and nothing could interfere with our connection or alter this majestic moment in any way. As I watched us, I did not look into our eyes or associate into my body or emotions, as that future conscious focus was meant to be experienced with each other in that moment to the fullest magnitude with pure, authentic expression and depth of emotion.

The audience is energetic and shares the excitement. As I joined the audience in the front right of the stage, I associated into their feelings and felt their collective excitement as they watched the proposal. I was moved to tears among the standing ovation from the audience, just as I saw myself moved to tears on stage as I accepted his proposal.

Golden light surrounds us on stage. The best moment, at the right time, was emphasized and amplified by the setting and the repeat previews in my mind. I feel his genuine love in my heart, growing and expanding, becoming ever-present just as it's meant to be always felt.

When he proposes to me, I authentically feel the experience in the moment because I've never associated into my body in advance of that moment. The moments of heightened emotional intensity are meant to be felt when they happen. I can see future emotional highlights and am not meant to step into my body and feel them in advance. I am meant to wait and experience them for the first time at their full intensity in the moment as the person I am then.

The defining moments of heightened emotional intensity and life-changing progress are meant to be experienced live and in that moment. We are meant to savor and experience those moments in our lives when their time arrives and in our present state as the person we are then. It's okay to preview. The previews are preparation. Foreseen events map the moments, providing highlights, markers, and energetic snapshots that light the way to keep us going toward our highest potential and the best moments to come. Just wait for the actual life event to feel the experience to the fullest extent.

Consider the moments you know will happen to be destinations in mind. Know that there is adventure and growth you are meant to experience along the way as preparation to reach the destination.

The stage proposal is one of my destinations that inspires me to keep moving in that direction. Some events are inspirational previews of great times ahead as we advance, knowing they will happen. Just wait to feel them when they happen. The emotions are meant to be felt for the first time as they occur and as the person you evolve into through your life experiences along the way. Give yourself the gift of waiting to feel the moments of heightened emotional intensity when their time arrives.

Chapter 18:

The Café is a Bridge

Bridges bring us together from separate places and connect us on our way. Some moments serve as bridges; the pivotal moments where we unite, deeply connect, and forge ahead strongly in the direction we are meant to go. There are some events where we can assist in advance to make sure our intentions, fate, destiny, and all forces connect us to our highest path and the life we are meant to lead together in unity. These bridges join us together, merging our consciousness and overcoming separation, and the seemingly impossible is accomplished.

Initially, the visions were involuntary and unconscious. I was an observer who entered unknowingly without expectation or intention of what would be observed. I could not direct my energetic placement within the vision. At first, it was uncomfortable to experience the level of intimacy that I was unfamiliar with at that point in my life. As the visions progressed, my perspective and level of openness changed, and I evolved.

The café is a metaphorical bridge I frequented. I had a vision of us at a café, staring into each other's eyes intensely as if the eyes were the connection point of our consciousnesses. It was in public as if we were the only people there. I recognized the café as if we had been there before. I was in my own body and felt slightly uncomfortable in this vision. I told him he would be in love with me if he kept staring at me, and he told me he already loved me. Then, I was out of my body, observing us, and back into my body, staring at him as he stared at me.

On another day, I had the vision again. We were staring at each other at the café. I could feel the flirtatious sincerity as we gazed into each other's eyes, projecting our energy to each other. We establish a connection of consciousness in the stare in complete rapport, maintaining eye contact and mirroring each other. I tell him we will be in love in the stare, and we agree that we already are. We were so alive and into each other. I could feel so much love shared between us growing and expanding as we stared at each other. We were both happy and into each other. The feeling continued as we left the café.

When we stare into each other's eyes, we increase our vibrational alignment, raise our vibration, and enhance the desired alignment. Eighteen seconds of focus locks us into energetic alignment, and with three seconds or more, we become drawn to each other. Love and allow it. As we gazed in silence, the silence held the intuitive telepathic power of our infinite connection. Looking deeply at each other, I could feel us connected through heart energy. We build rapport and soul connection love in this way.

More details became available as we touched each other's hands on the table. When we touched, I felt the energetic spark in my physical body as I watched the vision. Each time I entered the vision, I felt more, saw more, and was more open and receptive to the vision. The more open and receptive I became, the more I could see.

Eventually, I could consciously reenter the café vision.

Chapter 19:

Accessing Vista Points

Future visions are vista points highlighting great times ahead. At vista points, we stop and view where we are going. We see our destinations from a grand perspective, viewing from above and afar while we are removed from the scene. The way there may remain a mystery, but it gives us a clear perspective on where we are going.

All information across all timelines is available at every moment. It's just a matter of tuning into the channel. Imagine connecting with your heart and feeling the energy of your heart. Imagine the heart's energy expanding into light surrounding you. Take the light to a higher level as you elevate the heart's energy to your higher self and connect to your soul. Access your higher self in a place of supportive, unconditional love and go even higher to universal light and love. Bring in a golden glow of universal love and light. Surround yourself with that love and bring it into your body. Feel the universal love and light expand throughout your body.

From this place, ask about what you want to see. Enter a state of creative awareness: alert, calm, open, and perceptive. Watch the vision as it is revealed to you now. Focus upon the details as if viewing from various points within the scene. Maintain this state of creative awareness as you go about your day. Connect with your surroundings as more aspects of the vista point are revealed. Sometimes, intuitive information comes when you are not looking for it. Believe, trust, and know the information will come to you. Follow the clues to reveal more details about the destination.

Chapter 20:

Connection of Consciousness

Once you are strong in your energy, imagine connecting to the soul of another. Imagine sharing the universal light and love with them. Imagine you connect your heart's energy with theirs. Imagine moving the energy to your higher selves and your hearts and bodies. Then, radiate unconditional love back and forth to each other through your hearts and feel the merge of consciousness.

First, I imagined connecting our higher selves and souls, accessing universal light and love, projecting that light and love to our bodies, and surrounding our consciousness with golden light. Our higher consciousness raises the vibration of our living presence with the loving golden light. I set the intention to provide healing, and I imagined healing him by surrounding him in a golden, loving light and placing him in a healing bubble. I entered to penetrate his heart with unconditional, radiant, healing love.

I then imagined taking his consciousness to the café and showing him what I see. While there, he entered his body. At other times, he was the observer, along with me. We were across from each other, watching as we stared into each other's eyes.

The interchange of consciousness is within our eyes. We both entered each other's bodies. From my present state, in my bed, I could feel his body within mine. I could feel his suit jacket on his shoulders while I was in his body. I could feel his heart rhythm, body structure, openness, and curiosity. He was so excited about this new ability and wanted to see more.

I took him to watch us at the big stage event, where he introduced me as his beautiful wife to share the details with him, and as I entered the vision with him, I saw more details. He wore a gray suit on stage, and I wore a beautiful royal blue dress. He was smiling while he introduced me as his beautiful wife, Melissa Wild. We were on stage at an outdoor venue with a white-covered permanent fixture over the stage with a large-scale audience of 500+ people. We earn a significant amount of money from this one event. We each offer our perspective to the audience, and it is obvious that our vibrant dynamic is the foundation of our success.

He was excited with the freedom from his body and happy to share the good times ahead. He held my hand as we watched the stage event, and I could feel our consciousnesses having an interaction, while at the same time, I could feel it presently in my body. I could feel the love, accomplishment, and stability between us in our relationship. It felt good, calm, mature, and welcoming. We are both ready for our relationship to develop. He is intrigued by my precognitive abilities and connection to him. I appreciate the spiritual connection to him.

Staring into each other's eyes at the café and the feelings we feel as we watch each other on stage are two important moments in our love story. We watched the moment we consciously established a connection of consciousness and when we became successful. We watched each other and ourselves raising our vibration in love, and we experienced the excitement of our success. We savor and hold the moment.

The emotional moments are the key to accessing our timeline and knowing this is the life we want. These moments of heightened emotional intensity are meant to reveal highlights of the adventure, allowing us to be bold, brave, and authentic to keep momentum going along the path.

On these shared visions, the experience was kaleidoscopic, as multiple versions of us were present in fractals of our expanded consciousness, traveling beyond our daily awareness and watching ourselves along our timeline. First, we watched our future selves from a dissociated or out-of-body perspective. It was as if we were at the event, watching it from the back left corner of the venue.

Then we associated into our bodies in the version of us that watched, and as we watched, I felt the experience as we touched. It felt like I was in my body, sitting next to him in the vision. From there, I could feel a third version of myself—the current version of me feeling the touch in my present body. And this version of me felt him as if he were beside me in my bed even though we were geographically living a vast distance apart. The versions of our consciousness merged into one as we watched ourselves and each other in future events. We are meant to continue to emerge beyond what we know to be possible.

We share a mutual connection, a feeling, an inner knowing about what we collectively have together. We arose from our unconscious to conscious precognitive connection that links to our emotional shared experience. Dreams reveal to us who we are, showing what's next for us in our future together. We know it to be true. We have a beautiful relationship of genuine caring, effort, and prioritization, emphasizing how devoted and loving we are to one another.

Chapter 21:

Provocation of Connection

Future visions become accessible with a connection of consciousness. When I asked to see more, I envisioned a vibrant ball of white, translucent energy above my head. I felt warm and radiant love. While experiencing this feeling, I viewed photographic imagery of an aqua-blue ocean with sea lions in the Channel Islands that I had taken while snorkeling and an artistic aqua-blue image of a sea of flowers in the sky.

I wrote, "Keep the mystery alive. Allow it to unfold in its own time. Enjoy being within the mysterious adventure. The suspended animation of being between realities is a magical, weird, metaphysical time leading to everything wonderful. Beautiful, exotic adventures. Magnificent life beyond what is currently within view. The sea and flowers heal, magnify the light, and connect our consciousness of love."

I felt my consciousness spiraling from the ocean into a sea of flowers floating into the sky. The man of my dreams was with me in the water and above, directing me to him in the sky. It felt like hypnosis and was as familiar as previous dreams. I felt a sense of his human presence and his subconscious metaphysical energy as if there were multiple versions of him as a higher level of consciousness over me and expanding within my body. I watched as he floated above my spiral of consciousness within my body and then watched us from above as red and pink roses surrounded us.

It felt like he had conducted the same connection of consciousness technique I apply to mutually uplift our spirits and draw me up higher as I do to him. I could feel him in my physical body within the room, hypnotically as my protector and lover. I felt the love and genuine compassion in the connection. He shows love to my consciousness. The roses appeared as gratitude, just like the roses I sent him metaphysically in Reiki as a thank-you when we met last summer. I remember he thanked me when I told him I sent him roses.

A radiant, magnetic conscious experience of connection of us as our own universe, surrounding us in roses, uniting as one, spiraling to higher consciousness above where his higher astral body orchestrated our expertise. I felt the all-encompassing, fully present, shared connection in the most profound love. A deep yearning to experience this in the flesh with him was provoked, and a sense that he would keep courting me spiritually. A feeling of contentment peacefully resounded in knowing we shall unite soon in a hypnotic romance, a union that I eagerly await.

Chapter 22:

Expansive Future Visions

Continuing into my dreams, I viewed further along in our timeline. I saw us outside a desert home by the pool. Colorful red rocks were in the distance. It was a sunny day. We were facing each other, happily enjoying the day.

Just then, I associated into my body in the vision and looked at my hands in front of me. As we reached for each other, our hands appeared illuminated in golden light. Sparkling in the light, it was apparent that we were wearing shiny wedding rings. I felt excitement and anticipation at the sight of this future. The love and excitement amplified in my body as our hands touched and our fingers interlocked.

A collective vision of our future emerged, where we travel the world together. The vision appeared and progressed so fast, yet it felt infinite, providing vast details of future events. My vision began at a scenic overlook where we enjoyed the scenery along a mountainous coastal location. We were traveling up the mountain and had stopped to view the sea from a high vantage point. The location was vibrant, with homes in the mountains and easily accessible scenic overlooks from which to view the sea.

We were riding on two-wheeled motorized vehicles along the coast. The sea appeared aqua, and there were colorful flowers around us along the way. The flowers were pleasantly fragrant. The air was warm, and the ocean breeze felt exhilarating. The feeling of the place was lively and exuded romantic sensuality in atmosphere.

We then travel together to a tropical coastal location. Tropical vegetation grew on the mountains near the beach. We stayed in a private bungalow on the water with a private beach. From above, I could see us inside with me on top of him, riding him playfully and erotically as both of us enjoyed the pleasure. I felt the euphoric sensations in my physical body with just the glimpse of us. I watched from above as he entered the water, and as I jumped in, I felt the cool, refreshing water. The water was clear, and the coral was visible. We faced each other, treading in the water.

As we touched, I could hear the sound of the water, similar to the sound of our audience, so excited to listen to our story. Suddenly, I was brought back to the present, and as I washed my hands in the coconut soap, I could see my hands illuminated with golden light, his hands within mine, and his smile as he looked into my eyes. I felt calm, peaceful, and tranquil.

Chapter 23:

Collaborative Excitement

Our friends, who are so excited and want to be a part of the journey of us getting together, support us along the way. Sharing my story has built excitement and a genuine following of people who have become my closest friends and most supportive allies. Sharing brings a change of perspective.

A friend, Shazeela's excitement for me and supportive perspective helped me chill. She said he was taking the scenic route and reminded me that this was the last time I would ever have this experience. I thought of the mystery and the excitement of this metaphysical romance and the joy of getting to know him in real life. That shift changed everything and made me appreciate the perfect timing of our courtship. I savor the experience of us getting to know each other, beginning to love, and experiencing the progression of our relationship. I appreciate each day and joyfully anticipate all the wonderful times yet to come.

I was so excited when the hypnosis trainer gave me a coin that I told him the man of my dreams gave me one of these. Absent of context, he thought he was the man of my dreams. With a rush of excitement to clarify, I told him all the details about dreaming about this man for years, not knowing he was a person, and eventually figuring out he was someone I would meet. I told him that when we did meet, his hypnosis session took me right into one of the dreams I kept having.

He asked if this man was tall, dark, and handsome.

I replied, "No, blond hair, blue eyes, muscular."

He knew exactly who I was describing and told me the man of my dreams was his good friend, and he took a selfie of us and immediately texted it to him.

I was anxiously enthusiastic at that moment, wondering how the man of my dreams would respond. Obviously, he would realize that I was talking about him. I felt a little like, "Oh no! Now what?" We hadn't been in contact in a few weeks, and I could not believe that I had just told his good friend about the dreams and how much I liked him and that I see us creating something together that draws a big crowd based on our shared story, his charisma, and our magnetism.

He was so excited about the story that he planned to call him on his way home that night. I told him to put in a good word for me. Yet, I was slightly terrified, wondering what he would say to the man of my dreams because I was not shy about my feelings for him.

Soon after the conversation, the man of my dreams contacted me. He invited me to join his new adventure and asked me about the hypnosis training. I wondered what the hypnosis trainer told him, though I was not about to ask and acknowledge my conversation about him with his friend.

At some point, he transitioned the topic to sex. I kept it vague, as did he. I wanted to tell him how I felt about him, yet I was scared. I want us to have the best relationship, full of virtue and unconditional love, and I accept the scenic route.

We are off to a great start. We build our relationship slowly. Develop rapport and friendship and grow from there. Our friendship is beginning and becoming a deeper connection. There is more time ahead of us than we both have been alive.

Enjoy the scenic route.

Chapter 24:

Connection Across Time

I had a sense that he needed my help. So, I asked to enter a place where I could help him. I then put myself into a trance state. I saw an elderly version of him. In the vision, I joined him, appearing at my current age. I looked into his vibrant blue eyes and held his elderly hand. We connected telepathically, sharing moments and memories of one another. The older version of him and the current version of me watched our memories from above, viewing all around our bodies, enjoying the moment together and the memories we shared of his past and my future, all of which are our memories of our times together.

I showed him the excited emotional moments in my memories of when we first met. I showed him our first glance as we walked past each other while I was wearing the leopard print pants. Next, I showed him our initial meeting at the pool. I then showed him making eye contact with me as he read my face and our first hug. I showed him when he approached me, inviting me to hang out at the pool on our last day in Las Vegas.

He showed me events in his past and my future. We viewed times I hadn't seen yet, where we were at our desert home enjoying the warm weather and our backyard pool. It was a modern, almost futuristic place. He showed me a memory of a sexual experience in our desert home. It was a large bedroom with very high ceilings, almost as if we were outdoors. I was on top of him. His hands were on the bed, and his arms were back, holding him up. He was looking up into my eyes as I rode him, looking into his eyes. My hair was down, bouncing on my back as I rode him erotically. Our bodies were gorgeous and glowing, perfectly in sync as we sincerely enjoyed the pleasure. We were both healthy and in our prime.

We knew our relationship never ends and continues just as it began in the metaphysical realm, and our love continues infinitely. Love goes beyond physical boundaries. We felt the love emanating back and forth, vibrationally, tingling, and reciprocal across all points of the timeline. The strong mutual connection, attraction, and love intensified as we joined in unity on a journey to a higher vision. The intensity of our love was felt radiantly throughout our timelines, as love is timeless.

My perception of time changed as I established a connection of consciousness across past, present, and future timelines. We perceive and create our lives simultaneously. We are living among and within many timelines, all synchronously. It's never just a dream. We live on in another form of consciousness beyond where we are presently, where we are together on higher planes even now while our human forms are in other places, bodies separate, and souls united elsewhere above and beyond in places we sometimes experience small glimpses of.

Chapter 25:

To Get Healthy

Later that day in my waking life, I saw images on Pinterest of desert homes that looked just like the surreal home I saw in the dream. I thought about aligning frequencies, and it felt like a dream of him, so I texted him immediately. He asked me if I could access my intuition to help him to get healthy. He admires my intuition skills and has told me he wants to learn from me. He trusts in my abilities. I needed to help and committed to accessing my intuition to get him healthy.

I told him what I knew so far, everything from trust to veterinary drugs to dreams and a song. Over the following days, I told him everything exactly as it came to me. I shared the metaphors from my dreams and described what I saw when I scanned his body. Later that day, an image that looked like what I saw when I scanned his body came to my email. I sent that to him too.

I even shared that all else was sex dreams. We discussed our choice to be single and celibate and the rationale for our choices.

He has chosen to remain single and celibate while he completes a healthy, powerful, dynamic expedition. He won't allow any distractions. I chose celibacy to achieve energetic clarity and high vibration.

After that discussion, I received repetitive messages about attachments. One day, I suddenly had an intuitive insight that was so strong it made me dizzy, and I knew I had to share it with him immediately. Remove attachments. They like how you make them feel, and their attachment depletes you. Do an energy clearing.

That night, I dreamt of having a temporary relationship with someone I didn't care about and knew it would end badly. I could see the man of my dreams was very sick. I was trying to communicate telepathically to help him, guide him to wellness, and reassure him that he would get better. I realized we are connected, and our actions impact each other. Our communication was blocked. I must keep rejecting every man who is not him and commit to him now, even while we are just getting to know each other. He is the only man I allow into my energetic space. We will get through this together.

Chapter 26:

Healing Energy Connection

As we texted, I could see within and around his body energetically, similar to the experience when I scanned his body. There were insights I could not stop myself from sharing with him. I apologized because he had not asked me. I felt as if I had invaded his boundaries. He provided me with his consent.

I shared what I saw and felt regardless of how it was articulated. He let me know when he didn't know what I meant and asked me questions to understand me or learn more.

In the early morning, I was lying awake in bed when I could see him energetically. He appeared to be suffering. I willfully applied my healing abilities to help him. I accessed him from his higher consciousness to provide my support and raise his vibration of hope and strength. I saw our energies collectively expand in red, yellow, and golden light.

I then expanded my energy, increasing the frequency and size, projecting a shield around us. As my energy expanded, he became aware of my energetic presence as I surrounded him with healing energy. The stronger I am, the more I can help him through his higher self with my supportive, feminine, nurturing, healing energy to live his best life.

I fell asleep slightly, and our celebrity friend appeared in my dream. Dressed in costume, he handed me a tablet and told me to analyze the common truths hidden within various ancient texts as a way to help him. My mind analyzed the texts in multiple languages and symbols on various ancient formats on stone, wood, and old broken-down charred scrolls so rapidly that the core message was eloquently delivered deeply into my consciousness. Though I wasn't aware of the message, I trusted that I knew it.

As I woke up, a song was playing in my mind. I texted him the song and suggested he try something different and off the path. He told me that he was, and he had asked the universe to bring the path to him over a specific amount of time. Had my intuition come through as part of the intention he set?

The answer to the question is "Yes," and communicate my love for him with genuine, authentic expression. He is slow to trust, cautious, and analytical of every word due to past manipulation. What I know comes from a higher consciousness. He understands that and knows I have seen our future. He believes in me, relaxes, and trusts that I unconditionally and compassionately love him with genuine, authentic expression. He trusts that he is safe with me, feeling the warmth inside. I came through in a dark time as a source of inspiration and hope as his friend. He is curious to learn more about what I see.

Chapter 27:

Sharing Focused Intuition

Our relationship evolved as I accessed my intuition for him. We were open and ready to have the experience. I was no longer afraid to tell him exactly what I saw and no longer wondered if I should tell him. I knew I had to, so I texted him right as new information came. It was thrilling to have him to share my dreams and visions with, especially since he is the primary focus of my dreams. I cherished the dynamic of our relationship and the bold confidence I felt when sharing my perspective with him.

He began to share his intuitive visions with me. We see some of the same things. He told me he sees himself becoming a famous person on the big stage. I told him I see that too, and I see us both on stage. I told him he is next to me in some of the visions, watching future events with me. Sharing my intuition with him helped me focus on what I enjoyed most, and as I focused on what came easily, it became even more fun. I especially looked forward to sharing new information with him as it came.

One day, I was shopping at T.J. Maxx when I found that royal blue dress I saw myself wearing on stage with him. I was so overjoyed to find it that I took a selfie and texted him immediately. I couldn't wait to share it with him. "I found the dress from my dream. I love it when things come together." It took some courage to send a selfie of me wearing the dress. I felt shy about sending the image, wondering if it was inappropriate to send. All I could think was, *Proof, send him proof. That dress is significant in our story.* I sent the selfie and "My apologies in advance if that was inappropriate to send."

He loved the picture.

Later that day, he sent me one of his projects for my perspective. Some of his concepts were similar to my visions, and I wondered if we had the same visions and accessed the same content with our intuition. I understood his perspective more when I read his writing. My dreams have shown him just as focused as he is, and now I know, from his perspective, what we were doing in the dreams. We were previewing the good times ahead as we prepared for our future.

Chapter 28:

Astral Union

While focused on providing healing energy, I could see his energy expanding in white light, breaking away from red and black charcoal as he expanded. He approached me, inviting me to take his hand energetically, leave my body, and explore with him. Telepathically, he knew I was scared and intrigued and wanted to go with him. When I felt fear in this changing state, I felt his reassurance.

As I let go of my body and went to him, our energy bodies and consciousness merged as one. I could feel more intensely as I felt his heart within mine. I felt the warm, radiant, highly vibrational love intensify. Our love grows and expands beyond space and time. We vibrate higher together. Our relationship prevails infinitely and extends beyond conscious reality.

Our energy merged more frequently over time as he grew stronger, and I could see him as a golden glow of pure, energetic light. I felt our energy merge into red, yellow, and golden light with the intention to love, grow, heal, and evolve together in eternal love. I was finally ready to allow our union. I was focused entirely on him. He was the only thought on my mind, just as he had wanted all along, ever since the first dream he had entered.

We join together in strength with universal knowledge. We become more when we are together. The love from our souls is magnetizing, calling us to be together to share an infinite, intimate connection divinely summoned for a healing purpose. Focus on warm, radiant love from our higher selves and allow the most avant-garde, grandiose passionate relationship to evolve. The future is love.

The astral journeys sometimes came spontaneously and took me into the unknown. Light energy spiraled up through my body. I could feel my energy level rising. As my energy arose, I felt his consciousness approach and connect with mine. A warm feeling of radiant, vibrant yellow and red light and heat overtook my body. This light energy was transformational, a feeling of alignment on a higher vibrational level.

I could feel him merging within my body as the sensations overtook my body. There was complete focused concentration from both of us. As I became momentarily distracted by the noise in my environment, I heard his persistent desire to be the only one in my mind. He always wants to be my main focus. He is the only one I want to be with and to love.

When I released the resistance, I felt him and the connection of consciousness completely. As I focused on the connection, I could feel the love radiate through our eyes. A message carried through. Be ready for love. Travel of the mind is evolutionary for the soul reunion. Our union begins within our minds.

My dreams are as real as the physical world. Our consciousness brings them to our reality. Our higher connection of consciousness evolves our presence, bringing us to vibe higher together. Through our higher consciousness, we are becoming one in physical life. It manifests in dreams and in the urge to keep showing up.

Allow the desire, emotions, and physiological sensations of love to fill my heart, mind, and body in the physical world. Have patience. It's only a matter of time. Love is rising as a metaphysical force that magnetizes us to our union. We are always connected subconsciously. Stay on the frequency of unconditional love and virtue. Have compassion and experience joy.

Keep on and allow the astral union. Love is sharing in all the union's feelings: euphoric energy, intense emotion, and physiological sensations. The otherworldly feeling of being beyond our bodies, united on a higher plane of existence, merging as one. Allow the union of our magnificent connection on all dimensions.

I felt the energy changing colors as it spiraled through my body from the sacral chakra in red to yellow and orange in the solar plexus to green in the heart, blue in the throat, and indigo in the crown. Just as the energy released, I felt a total body liberation and an exchange of collective euphoric sensations overtake my body. I could then feel his masculine, protective love merge within my energy. A collaborative cloud of red, yellow, and white stars surrounded our consciousness.

I felt it at a higher level and simultaneously within my physical body. As my physical body had the experience, all became one. Wherever the mind, body, and spirit may be, all can connect in unison. The astral metaphysical experiences bring us together on the Earth plane.

Keep allowing the activation and enhancement of these experiences. Be all in. Allow it to expand. This brings us together on all levels in all ways. The love we share and how we found each other is a miracle. Our relationship builds on the astral plane through our connection of consciousness.

Chapter 29:

An Ancient Tree on a Walk Among Growth

While walking through the woods at night for a change of perspective, with no destination or idea of where I would end up or what I would experience, I happened upon an ancient tree. I was intrigued when I noticed rusty old barbed wire wrapped around a limb, appearing as if it had grown into the tree. The tree continued to grow regardless of the restriction of the barbed wire. When I touched the barbed wire, it just broke away, crumbled, and decayed into pieces. As the barbed wire fell away from the tree, it occurred to me the barrier is an illusion, and it is easy to remove.

Questions entered my mind. What in your life appears as a restriction that could easily fall away? What could easily be removed? Where have you grown as a result of a perceived restriction? Where are you most resilient? Where are you so naturally persistent that no perceived restriction will limit your growth or progress?

I took a picture of the tree to reflect upon later. When I looked at the picture, it appeared as if eyes were looking out from inside a hole in the tree. Initially, the image made me think of the devil tarot card. Some limitations are an illusion. Remove the bondage that is in the way.

That night, I dreamt of tarot cards. The world appeared as a smiley face with a crown of thorns. In the dream, the card symbolized the completion of a cycle and the end of a journey from the past.

He reached out to me that morning, and I shared the image with him. He was interested in the metaphors, dreams, and meanings associated with my experience. At the time, I was still working with him to heal, and I wondered if the message was meant for him or both of us. Eventually, upon further reflection, I realized the tree provided universally applicable insights. The tree supported life. Actions of supportive, unconditional love are the way forward.

Months later, I shared the image in a conference presentation and the story of my walk in the woods and asked the audience questions. The virtual walk with my audience continued along with more questions. And as the journey continued, I shared that I could feel rocks under my feet and felt compelled to find and balance some rocks in the dark. To balance rocks, first the rocks must speak to you. The rocks must also click with each other. You get a feeling, and they click. What or who are your rocks? How do you feel when they click? Where is your life well balanced?

As the walk continued into the day, we noticed various fungi and ground pines growing. Even in the midst of winter, so much life and growth thrive together within the forest. In what areas of your life are you growing? Whom are you thriving with or among? Where do you feel the deepest connection?

Chapter 30:

Creation of Our Future

We support and nurture each other's growth and energize each other's vibrational expression. We are building a strong foundation for living our lives together in a harmonious union. We create our best life together, expressing our highest capabilities. Combining our talents and skills results in building collaboratively to launch together collectively. Our unique creative genius and enlightening future vision will occur in different backgrounds as we travel and present all over the world together and generate a high financial income. Together, we achieve massive wealth. True wealth comes from connection that is cultivated like a garden.

We are on our own frequency and in our own universe. We are magnetic, radiant souls with a deep love for each other, knowing we are meant for each other and fated to be together. We feel the magnetic attraction pulling us closer, and as we come together, the force becomes stronger. Together, we rise. We amplify one another vibrantly in virtue and unconditional love, feeling our hearts magnetically together in our souls and higher selves. We have a transformational soul purpose to fulfill. We will live our reciprocal dream state imagined in real time as life. We will excel together and collaboratively live the authentic life of our shared dreams. We are sensational together. Love surrounds us. Love enhances everything in our lives.

Keep feeling the warm, mushy, gut-wrenching, euphoric feelings of love. Graciously accept and reciprocate the emotional intensity. Explore ecstasy and the exotic depth of romantic connection. He's romantic and desires a deep connection. He is focused on me. Be confident and believe in my dreams. Authenticity aligns us. We have a harmonious relationship with enduring prosperity. Staying in the action of intuition is what gets us there. We become more bonded to each other with each event we share, with all positive thoughts and intentions for each other and our life together on this love adventure.

We are important to each other. Help him be confident by being confident in his dream. He acknowledges our connection and wants my influence in his life. I was delighted when he chose to share his projects with me and asked for my feedback. I was so excited that I reviewed the contents three times to give him comprehensive and cohesive, detailed feedback. He valued my perspective and contacted me for input on several additional projects.

I imagined projecting unconditional love as I connected our hearts to see the details of what we create together. Our story of how we met is magical and magnetic. The celibacy chosen along our path to unity is the key to our success in love and business. We are meant to love each other and share our passion with our audience. Our love attracts a crowd and more love. Feel into that love. Allow it. Receive it. Accept it graciously. Sharing our story raises people's vibrations with hope. We uplift people and will provide healing to others.

We will help singles open their hearts, connect with their souls, and develop themselves to dream of and energetically attract their soulmates. I will show individuals how to connect with the higher self of their ideal mate and get to know them on a higher level while developing themselves and living their most authentic life to be ready for their ideal mate to appear in their life.

We will apply my psychic connection with his charismatic attraction to help people attract and recognize their best partnerships and live their best lives. We will help couples strengthen their relationships. Relationships strengthen when couples connect intuitively. We host an event for couples to deepen their connection. We will help individuals connect with their higher selves and build their intuition to attract what they desire on a higher level. Everyone benefits most when doing what brings them the most divine joy, light, and freedom.

Chapter 31:

When Past Meets Present

I love to focus on what's next, and the songs continue to foreshadow my life, lead me to where I am meant to go, and cause me to pay attention to those moments. I was packing for my trip to San Diego when I heard "Graduation (Friends Forever)" by Vitamin C playing and felt nostalgic happiness from within.

The next day, at the gate for my flight, I heard a name called. It was the name of my high school boyfriend. And yes, he, too, has blond hair and blue eyes. We were scheduled for the same flight. I approached him, and we talked while waiting for our flight. We reunited at our layover in Detroit and talked for three hours. We picked up right where we left off years ago and caught up on our lives beyond high school, everything up until now, including updates on our families and future plans. It was as if no time had elapsed, even though we realized we had not seen each other in twenty-three years.

I realized I was meant to have this unplanned and unexpected reunion to remember who I was and where I was going. The song guided me to step into this moment. I felt safe and comfortable talking to him, and it was a reminder of how important friendship and intellectual conversation are to me in a relationship. He was always calm and treated me with respect. Stability and maturity are essential on my way forward. He is in a wonderful marriage, and I feel genuinely happy for him.

I had been thinking a lot about Valentine's Day when I was around fourteen years old. I saw him approaching me as I walked to science class. He was carrying one red rose, and he looked so happy. I felt butterflies and excitement and was overcome with fear. I ran away and didn't see him again that day.

This was the first time I ran away from a moment of heightened emotional intensity, and it was by far not the last, just the beginning of a pattern. I always felt bad for running away from him, and I really liked him back then. Our relationship did not end based on my fear; I remember we talked on the phone later that day. Our relationship continued, and we remained friends throughout high school. We worked together as lifeguards in the summers. I never apologized for running away and don't believe he saw me run. Serendipitously, I believe seeing him at the airport gave me closure.

I had a sudden epiphany about running away from the moment of heightened emotional intensity that I saw coming when I was fourteen. Guarding my emotions caused me to wait to have the most dramatic, virgin, and unadulterated moments of heightened emotional intensity of my life with the man of my dreams. The moment when asked to spend my life with him will have even more wild intensity than the moment I ran away from.

We must allow and trust love. Surrender self-sabotage, fear, and running by showing up, leaning in, being honest and vulnerable, tender and compassionate, and accepting love with pure, heightened emotional intensity. I look forward to showing up for the most deeply heartfelt moments yet to be revealed and experienced with him. I feel such a resounding desire to lean into the purity of love as it presents itself to me in the future.

I once shared the message with the man of my dreams, "We are not meant to associate into the moments of heightened emotional intensity; we are meant to experience them for the first time as the person we are then."

Now, I realize I was also meant to wait to experience the most highly vibrational moment of heightened emotional intensity not only as the person I become but with the person I am in the highest vibrational alignment with.

Chapter 32:

Like A Movie Scene

In flight, I watched the *Barbie* movie and was struck unexpectedly with annoyance. I related to the Santa Monica scene in the movie where men made provocative comments to her, wanting to touch and play with her like a doll. This scene resonated with me as it mirrored the offensive behavior I've experienced in my life. I feel disgusted and unsafe around people who do this to me, and it began as a child. As a redhead, I've always received a lot of unwanted attention. I related to the movie's depiction of the doll's life, where everyone wants to touch and play with you, and it's offensive.

Later that day, I signed in at the simulation conference, where I was presenting a session. As I walked through a building, I felt something touch my hair. No one was around me, and there was no breeze as I was inside. It felt like a warning, and I was on guard. About an hour later, while seated in the keynote conference room, the man sitting next to me reached over and intentionally touched my hair. I rejected this character. Reject everything that stands in the way to allow the space for the creation of what's meant to be.

All this unwanted attention has been a problem everywhere I go. The time to stop it is here and now. It was time to take control of the situation. But how? I keep rejecting them. For quite some time, my life has felt like I have been living in a zombie movie scene, and these men are the zombies running at me from every direction, and I enter constant combat defense mode, fending them off. This is the time to demolish any blocks and work through any challenges. I felt this was the final step in my freedom, knowing that I am safe and that I choose who touches me and what language and behavior I accept from others.

The keynote speech on the final day of the conference provided further insight. Something within me resonated with the toxic attention as if it was the only attention I would get, and that cycle is done because I know it is false. There is a better way. I remembered the Limp Bizkit concert where I was invited to dance on stage. I felt like a rock star! That was the attention I wanted, to be on stage and untouchable. I was 100 percent strong and authentic, and that woman exists within me. Bring her forth and liberate her. Set her free to thrive on that stage and in the spotlight with all eyes on me. Choose how I receive attention.

As I show up authentically, he is attracted to me magnetically. We are minutes to union, connection, and oneness for all of life. The final confirmation came as I walked through the hotel café. I heard, "For what it's worth, I'll protect you. I'll love you." In that moment, I realized I won't run or fight anymore because I am safe.

Chapter 33:

Spontaneous Visions of Future Memories

As I remembered that sequence of songs of his intentions, I heard, "I want you to be my wife." We unite and celebrate in unconditional love and balanced harmony as soulmates with deep and reliable commitment, stability, and security. We honor, support, and protect each other for life. We join together in sacred marriage, together as husband and wife for over forty-four years. We are a solid team, deeply in love and supportive of one another. We build each other up. We excel together and transform each other's lives.

As I walked down the runway aisle, I had a future memory of us as we walked down the runway aisle. I saw a flash of us boarding a plane and walking along a tropical, humid destination with bamboo and dense, lush vegetation. I saw quick flashes of our travel to hot tropical locations. I felt happiness as we traveled to the destinations revealed in my dreams. Glamorous, exciting, romantic travel awaits in our adventurous relationship. We travel the world together in love.

One morning, I woke up to palindromes, a rapid sequence of visions, and a message to review my notebooks. It was as if I had been given advanced knowledge and documented the dreams in the notebooks, and I was not supposed to be privy to that knowledge, but it was already given to me. So, I read the notebooks and remembered additional details from prior future visions. The open-air arena is in Australia. We make $500k from that event. We design a protocol in collaboration, and our cohesive, energetic dynamic is magnetically attractive. We create a healing technique. Love and massive wealth surround us more than anything we have ever known or anticipated. We show up for each other. We are going to rock this life together beginning right now.

Our Immediate Future

The man of my dreams sent me book suggestions before my trip to San Diego, and the intuitive messages flowed as I read them. Allow the flow of what I am doing to lead me to where I intend to go. Our life together is taking shape now. Collaborate and co-create. Build our intellectually stimulating and growth-enhancing partnership. Incubation is a time of gestation. Allow it to flow naturally, and he will "Run To You" by Bryan Adams, and that time is nonstop Vegas. The destination is our sensation. I was enchanted with the feeling he's into me, and he wants to dance with me.

Suddenly, I felt I had entered a memory of us staring into each other's eyes in the elevator, but it was a vision of the future, and I was not within my body. The vision came with principles of insight. Eye contact is an expression of love. Our eyes are how we connect and show love. When we look into each other's eyes, we establish an instantaneous connection of consciousness. We are ready for fate, free will, and destiny to meet.

I could see us staring into each other's eyes, knowing that we knew staring into each other's eyes brings us closer and raises our vibration of love. I watched us leave the elevator and walk toward my hotel room. As we walked, I could feel our vibration increasing, and I knew we were about to share our first kiss. I have previewed the scene of our first kiss before, but never the moments leading up to it. I have seen this kiss occur outside my hotel room. This is the final first kiss for both of us, an experience to savor.

As I watched and as our lips touched, I felt a euphoric tingling sensation throughout my entire body. Even though I had not associated into my body, the intensity of the kiss carried through to my body in the moment of the vision. As I felt the vibrational connection of consciousness across time, I could see that we would always be together and that I would tell him this with complete confidence.

And as I wrote about this vision, I entered another part of the vision immediately preceding the elevator scene. I realized our first kiss occurs after we leave the café together. In the café, he asks me what's next.

I tell him, "We leave here together, stare into each other's eyes in the elevator, and get off on my floor. We will share our first kiss in front of my room. Beyond that, it is all up to you."

During this vision, a Spanish song played in my mind. The upbeat tone, rhythm, and laughter within the song provoked a feeling of sexual attraction, passion, fun, and playful excitement for what's to come. The lyrics roughly translated into my mind to reveal a message: "If you love me, I will run away with you. I am ready for my destiny." He will choose the path. He wants to touch my hair. I could see smiles, laughter, and gentle, close touching. Let love flow. Be open to the experience and have fun along the way. I felt excitement in anticipation of the times ahead.

Our relationship will evolve to the next level. Additional Spanish lyrics translated to "I will elope with you." I thought, *No way, not a word I use or how either of us acts.* The next song, "Marry You," by Bruno Mars, reinforced the uplifting, lighthearted, fun outcome we have to look forward to.

Before receiving the songs in Spanish, I remembered a discussion with him about internal voice. I thought about how my internal voice comes in the form of music. He suggested changing the channel, and it sounded like I changed the channel to Spanish. Regardless of the language and whether or not I understood all the words spoken, I felt the feelings within the upbeat tone and rhythm.

When he reached out the following day, I thanked him for suggesting changing the channel; now, I am getting songs in Spanish. I told him the song was aligned and congruent with the other messages and awakened sexual feelings. Over the following days, I felt so much sexual tension. The songs that played were about sexual attraction, hypnotizing and mesmerizing. The moment we look into each other's eyes, we know. A complete connection of consciousness is what we experience together, hypnotized as we stare into each other's eyes.

Chapter 34:

On Sharing the Dreams

We discussed him being the same in my dreams as he is in real life, which encourages me to keep showing up. He asked if I would tell him if he is ever off the path of the man he is in my dreams.

My dreams show us together, married, living a life of travel, and presenting on the big stages. I wondered if this was the path he wanted to take. I asked him which path he wants to be on. He wants to be on his authentic path. He said he didn't know what I saw and that he would like to see what I see. I told him, "Someday, I will share all my future visions with you. More has to actually happen first, as in more confirmations."

He loved that.

The closer we became, the more I wanted to tell him what I saw and how I felt. I remember he once told me, "Melissa, we are going to travel the world together."

I responded, "I know we will. I have seen it in my dreams, and they always come true." I had already told him about seeing us on stage together. I have yet to share the deeper context of our relationship with him. We are married in the future visions.

One morning, I figured out when and how I would share all my future visions with him. When we are together in person, I am going to take him to the visions where he is next to me, watching future events. He has always been in those visions with me because I take him there and share the visions with him. I see us lying on the hotel bed with his hand in mine as I vividly describe the visions and teach him how to dissociate from his body.

We expand our energies beyond our bodies, becoming the purple, pink, and blue geometric clouds of consciousness. I describe the energetic freedom, expansion, unconditional love, and light surrounding us in all dimensions. I vividly enhance the euphoric feelings within and beyond our bodies, and we feel them completely. Then I take him to the vision I had on the plane where we are on the big stage. I am wearing the royal blue dress I sent him a picture of, and show him introducing me as his beautiful wife.

We feel our feelings as visitors to this place at a time when we are successful on the big stage. He sees the future dynamic of our relationship and experiences his feelings as he watches this with me from the audience. He takes my hand as he sits next to me, watching, and we approach for a closer look from the stage. Our energy is magnetically connected, impenetrable by outside forces, including this past version of us.

As our hands touch, we feel the emotions of bliss, happiness, excitement, and love tingling throughout our bodies.

We feel all levels and versions of ourselves now and in the future. We feel the euphoric state in our bodies now in the present together, feeling exhilarated to see us together in the future.

As we feel these feelings energetically, we bring our emotions and physiological sensations into the present. As I awaken his consciousness, returning him to his physical body, he feels my hand within his, completely loving this shared vision and continuing to feel the exhilaration. The emotions and physiological sensations remain in our bodies as we experience our wakeful consciousness. Whenever we think of the vision, we feel the emotions and physiological sensations and know we live our best lives together.

We have romantic, passionate, emotional bonding, wild, erotic, and euphoric sex as this metaphysical journey concludes, and our connection is solidified. The passionate attraction is so intense that it occurs in slow motion as we feel every detail of euphoric pleasure. I feel him, and I feel us emotionally, physically, energetically, and physiologically as we enjoy loving and pleasuring each other, feeling all the feelings with wild intensity.

This is the most erotic experience of my entire life, and I know this is our beginning, and it keeps getting even more amazing as our relationship progresses. As our connection of consciousness emerges into our physical reality, we transcend beyond our waking consciousness, beyond our bodies, beyond time, and we emerge together as one, feeling the euphoria and bringing the sensations into our waking level of conscious reality.

Chapter 35:

Magical Manifestation of Desire

He persistently asked, "What do you desire?" I tuned in and felt the feelings within my body. I want you. All I could think was, I want to live my life with you. I desire a life with you and know from my dreams that you are the direction I am meant to go. I am meant to proceed in my life with you, the man I've always dreamed of. I want to see all my wonderful dreams come to life with you.

My deepest dreams have become my desires. The more he showed up in my dreams, the more I desired him. The more I got to know him, the more it was apparent to me that he was exactly as he was in my dreams. I love that he's just like he is in my dreams. I felt grateful for all my dreams, visions, songs, intuition, and all the sources that showed me and led me to the man of my dreams.

The more energy I focused, the more clearly I could see our loving relationship. Wisdom and clear focus are the channels for manifesting our union. The action steps were obvious as I focused intently on the direction I most want to go. Self-confidence and action are essential. Be brave and confident in my communication. Speak up now. Communicate with authenticity. Speak my true feelings to those I love. Always be true to myself at all times. Advance with certainty and strength toward my highest unity-conscious love.

His words to me in real life were the same as those I had written in the messages about my dreams. What we see and what we feel is what we will create. We will manifest what I see in my dreams. If I see it in my mind, it will happen in my life.

The dreams revealed our future memories. We experience tremendous love and bliss in our future together. This time is coming upon us now. Sharing glimpses of our future gives us hope and joy in what's to come as we build our lives in the present. Seeing us in advance gave me the momentum to keep showing up in real life and have the experiences with him.

His support in real life mirrored my dreams, as he continued to be as supportive as he was in my dreams. He was excited for me when I shared my email about being asked to be on the planning team for the Creativity Expert Exchange. Our conversation sparked a realization and amplified the manifestation of all the little things. I manifested a shark pinata for a Cinco de Mayo retirement party, a panda plant, and a soulmate crystal. It was as if I became more powerful with his suggestion.

I appreciated him and knew definitively that I wanted a relationship with him. Thank you for giving me hope and showing me what I most want in my life: a reciprocal, loving relationship with you. I love you.

I wrote: "The future with the man of my dreams is happening right now, as we are. I see it now because it's now. Be grateful."

As I wrote, I heard him say, "Take action as you see the way unfold naturally before you."

We are balanced and in tune; our unconditional love, intuition, and mystical connection reveal what is hidden and true. We are manifesting the dream of ideal love, abundance, and fulfillment in our relationship and business.

Chapter 36:

Telepathy Along the Way

One afternoon, I felt overtaken by fear. As much as I desire the life with the man of my dreams, I understand that it will require me to embrace a new chapter, leaving behind the life I've known to move forward in our relationship.

Our time together is sacred, to be cherished, and must not be put on hold. It will happen so fast that it is as if there is no time to pack or say goodbye to our current lives as we know them. We will have to say goodbye to our current lives to love and live our lives together.

As I fell asleep, his voice echoed in my mind. It was as if I was back in my original dreams, where he urged me to follow my heart and pursue what I truly desired. His words provided a comforting reassurance, encouraging me to let go of any fear and trust in the path I was destined to take. I could hear his voice in my thoughts, guiding me. I felt a sense of calm as I tried to tune into his message. I reached out for his hand energetically, and I could feel his energy in the palm of my right hand. This feeling lingered as I drifted into sleep.

The way feels like a staircase along a steep, jagged trail with switchbacks where significant steps and incremental changes need to be made at precise moments as they occur. These are the things I cannot yet see, and they are coming up very fast. The way is rigorous and short. I could not make a plan because necessary details were missing. I could see jagged, short, steep stairs on a dirt path as a metaphor for the way. We are almost there. It is a short, steep path with many difficult decisions. I am on the path. Keep going. Take the dusty uphill climb and go where I want to be.

There are things we both need to do before we are ready to be together. He will come to me when the time is right. The songs on my morning commute brought a feeling of happiness and acknowledgment as if a sense of telepathic communication of his thoughts. He thinks I'm magical and different from anyone he has met before. I stand out. He believes in my skills beyond what I even thought possible. He likes that I'm a little bit older than him. He goes deeply into his relationships and will be devoted to me. We are friends now, building a foundation of supportive commitment. First, he is building his business and doesn't want to short-circuit his business or me, so he is finishing what he started, and when he is ready, he will be all in with me.

He approaches relationships with wild intensity. His devotion is beyond what I have previewed or experienced in my dreams. He wants me to know, just like the preview of his content, the same goes for dreams; they are a preview of our incredible life together. We will have plenty of time to enjoy each other and our endlessly changing horizon as we travel the world together.

The dreams were preparing me to be open and receptive to the wild intensity of his love. We will take each other places spiritually, mentally, emotionally, and physically. We have the rest of our lives to create and explore together.

Chapter 37:

Like a Marble Sculpture

One night, within a dream, I entered the scene of my first solo, out-of-the-country vacation ten years prior. This time, he was there with me. At first, I thought it would be like the original dreams, where he was taking me to the circumstances leading up to that trip. However, he assured me he was not there to visit the past. He was there to move forward with me. He was there as a protector, to keep me safe and wanting to spend time with me. Our desire to spend time together was mutual. I felt safe with him.

As we walked along at night, viewing marble sculptures, he had his arms around me, holding me tightly and hugging me around my waist. The contact felt clingy and different from my life experience thus far, as if it would take time for me to become accustomed to having so much public physical contact. It was apparent that physical contact is an essential connection for him.

I reciprocated the hug, and as we held each other tightly, it felt like we were beginning to adhere, melding into one. The longer we held on establishing the strong bond of connection, the more tightly we adhered, as if we were solidifying into one marble sculpture of the two of us. I could feel the physical contact as strongly as if he was with me. The physical connection was building strongly as the dreams evolved.

We mutually and equally felt the pull of attraction like an adhesive unifying us together as we became rock solid, strong, and indestructible. When we unite in physical form and touch, the adhesive attraction takes full effect. We know it and want it and will seek it out. We put equal effort into making the connection, and once we do, natural forces of momentum solidify us. We are stable, safe, and secure together. He will turn up the charm and deliver love. We join together in confident action and balanced intuitive partnership. It will be peaceful and celebratory when we unite and join our worlds as one, connected in spirit, mind, heart, and body.

Mastering the power of our minds, we merge and blend our divine intellect to achieve harmony. In our connection of consciousness, we display excellence and make a lasting monumental impact. Our dynamic symbolizes wisdom, strength, and durability across time. We know we belong together. As we remain connected, the adhesive will solidify as we both want. Persistent, focused attention over time formulates a sculpture of perfection. He feels the push-pull attraction and hesitation that I feel, as well as the fear and desire for eternal perfection, with the spotlight on us.

As we walked along, the scene progressed to the present and into a future vacation. While viewing white marble sculptures, one sculpture looked like a model of us. Together, we are like a beautiful marble sculpture displaying lasting beauty and intrigue in the intricate details and time spent manifesting monumental perfection. As we support each other in health, stability, and solid structural growth and formation, we become a power couple, perfected slowly with care and precision over time.

Actual Presentation

My dreams about him keep coming true. The initial real-life presentation provides fascinating details that incite me to continue the adventure. I had the idea to lie face down in the snow. It was such an exhilarating experience that I did it several times, even in my bikini top. The impression in the snow displayed the details of my facial features, including my hair, eyebrows, nose, lips, and the structure of my cheekbones and jawline. My bikini top was outlined and even showed cleavage and my bone structure.

Fascinated by the detail, I took pictures of the mold of my body in the snow. That night, I took photos of the full moon through a scope in preparation for the total solar eclipse. When I looked at the pictures side by side, it was apparent that the night sky image and my body's white impression in the snow were symbolic representations of the dream.

Later that day, I got chills at the confirmation I received as I remembered the unexpected hugs he gave me when I approached him and told him he was the man of my dreams. The spontaneous hugs were a genuine expression of love. Suddenly, I realized as soon as we touched, we were awakened like a picture come to life.

Chapter 38:

Courageous Self-Expression

Imagine awakening within a beautiful painting, and everything is enhanced beyond typical waking reality. Walking within brightly colored, vibrant imagery animated with movement across the sky and among the scenery, I was awake within a dream, knowing I was in the combined scene of an astrological painting and the Star tarot card.

The scenery to the left represented the past, and the scenery to the right represented the future. I stood in the middle, in the present, and as I immersed myself within the present scene, the past became smaller. The future blended with the present scene until it was all one vibrant, lively, magical world. This world had a clear message. The time is always now. Everything is happening now. Life is vibrant now. I have found the ideal love and the fantasy world where I aspire to live. The dream showed the expansion of the world in vibrant colors, rising up and being happy and feeling fulfillment in a successful, loving relationship with all of life.

The Star tarot card symbolizes truth revealed, ideal love, and the realization of a dream. Self-belief is essential. I know that I will succeed and continue to apply the internal navigation of my intuition. Express myself. Success in love is coming. Create opportunities and manifest the happy relationship and fulfillment in love as if we are alive within a beautiful dream of vibrantly colorful artwork.

The words from a familiar song were articulated in my mind but in a different voice. While browsing social media, those words appeared on a shirt for the total solar eclipse. The image on the shirt resembled the artwork I entered in the dream. The dream symbolized awakening, expanding beyond perceived boundaries, and experiencing life's vibrant, colorful aspects.

Then, I researched until I found the covered version of the song and listened to "The Sound of Silence" performed by Disturbed. The beat of this remixed version was like the music playing loudly in Las Vegas, and as the song played, it felt like my brain was synchronizing with the rhythm. It was apparent that this was the song I was meant to listen to. The song continued to play loudly within my mind, pulsating through my entire body and nudging me to the bold action of courageous self-expression.

He asked me to join his class, and when I received the intake form, I was so brutally honest and vulnerable that I felt anxious about admitting my struggle with self-worth. I acknowledged harshly critiquing my body, academic credentials, and where I live. I shared the desire to build my confidence and my desire for self-expression to tell the whole story. I even admitted to how I have struggled to talk by choking on the words, feeling my chest tighten and my throat constrict, and holding back only telling part of the story. I want the confidence to clearly articulate the whole story.

All the things that I felt insecure about admitting to the confident man of my dreams, whom I prefer to see me at my best, were revealed on this intake form. I had just let him into the most vulnerable insecurity within my mind. I admitted things I prefer not to admit, even to myself, because I want to overcome everything that holds me back to live my best life entirely. I want to experience the best outcome as revealed in my dreams, and I want to experience what I have yet to articulate to him.

I have yet to reveal the actual destined outcome and the most significant part of the story with him, and I want to share the outcome with him. The outcome: Tell the man of my dreams all the visions I have for us without waiting for any more confirmations. I know what I know. I want to share everything with him, every detail of every dream I have of us. I want to tell him how I feel about him and that I want the relationship with him that I see in my dreams.

My courageous self-expression happened in an unexpected way. I was so excited that my new bikini arrived in the mail as we texted about an upcoming conference in Las Vegas. I tried it on and texted him about how it looked. "It is Vegas-worthy, though definitely not ocean-worthy. Skimpy is fine for the pool. I need something tight and with more coverage so I'm not falling out of the cups in the ocean. Female fashion challenges…"

He had no clue what I was talking about and I refrained from sending him a picture.

Chapter 39:

Silent Moves of a Past Life

In the early morning hours, I was awoken within a dream, looking through my own eyes at the way to freedom. I felt the rigor and intense aspiration of walking and crawling across a rickety old railroad trestle bridge. The bridge was broken in a large section over a high ravine. A few blackened wood beams remained as the single connecting path across the bridge to freedom. I had to climb down a short section, crawl across a single beam, and climb up to the remaining intact section of the bridge. I could feel the roughness of the beams on the palms of my hands as I climbed.

I felt confident in my physical strength and agility, knowing I would successfully make it across. There was no way back, as the territory and circumstances behind me were unsafe and more dangerous than the bridge. Though I knew it would be a fatal fall if I slipped, I felt safe, as if there was an invisible field of protection around this section, and I forged ahead, making my way to the land.

When I arrived on the land, there were three men dressed in wool uniforms. As I approached these men, I had to express my honest intentions about where I was going and what I hoped to find. I was scared but knew this was the final step to freedom. I pointed in his direction and told the men I was going to unite with him. I was advised that he was their general. I could see his resemblance in the distance and recognized him immediately.

As soon as I saw him, I felt physical sensations and emotions running throughout my body. As he approached me and we looked into each other's eyes, I could see a look of attraction and recognition as if across time and consciousness. It was evident that we knew each other in that life, and in that moment, I felt safe and knew we would succeed.

His appearance was different from the way he currently appears. I also did not appear as I currently do. We lived in a prior era during a turbulent time in the United States. The men were soldiers, and I was escaping to freedom along the underground railroad. The soldiers and others on the path were all striving to achieve freedom and, collectively, liberation for all humanity. We worked individually to the best of our capacity and collectively to keep each other safe along the way. There was a spiritual erudition of abolition as long as we remained firm in our beliefs and consistent in our actions.

It was apparent that this was the lived experience of our past lives; one where we may have been forbidden from having a relationship. It was evident we knew each other and were, at minimum, working together for the same purpose. This was a life where our freedom was not promised. A life where he was mandated into service, and I was fighting for freedom to live a life of my own choosing.

As time passes and we become more distant from the past, we lose sight of the challenges and sacrifices of those who came before us until one day, when we have the experience of seeing small glimpses that remind us of where we were and where we are going. Our choices are up to us at this fortunate time to be alive.

We owe it to ourselves and each other to move forward together in unity. Acknowledge all that we have overcome in our own lives and all that our collective consciousnesses did to lead the way to allow us to live in freedom to choose the life we desire. Be grateful to the collective evolution of humanity and continue to evolve harmoniously. History carries through to the present, and we must move forward with bold action. Evolve and heal the pain carried energetically throughout the lifetimes. See the path ahead and lead the way in honor of the strengths given to us through our lifetimes.

King of the Dock

There have been plenty of times in my life when I have remained quiet. Yet, I have never failed to take action. There are other ways to communicate beyond verbal expression. Move in silence and take strategic action in the direction I want to go.

I remember being feisty and bold, physically active, and always on the move as a youth. I always performed well athletically and never hesitated to show off my athletic abilities. I could outrun and outswim all the boys. While swimming in the pond, I won every race and always won King of the Dock. I remember throwing the blond-haired, blue-eyed boys off the dock, jumping off the dock, swimming after them, and pulling them under the water.

Physical strength and agility were always my strengths. I have always been confident and bold in my physical body performance and have maintained my physique and strength throughout my life. In the water, my confidence and inner redheaded fighter comes to the surface. My strength is apparent in my most highly resourceful state, and I always win.

What My Notes Revealed

Seven years before we met, I wrote: "Blond man dreams: A voice told me to go and do the activities I am interested in, and I will meet him there." Naturally, we would meet at the pool; swimming is my greatest interest and being in the water is my most confident place.

Love Note

I've preferred blond hair and blue eyes since elementary school. In my memory, I saw that I knew his name when I learned to write. I had written his name in my youthful handwriting on lined Manila paper where I learned margins and zones. I wrote him a love note, folded it, and placed it inside my desk.

We were not allowed to write love notes in second grade. The teacher found the note and made me take the note from the desk and read it out loud to the class. I was shy, and reading that note to my entire class was terrifying. My face felt hot, and I knew it was as red as my hair.

The spotlight was on me. I remember the looks on the faces of my classmates. The boys looked horrified and relieved that the description was not of one of them. The girls appeared jealously intimidated by my bold audacity and courageous public expression. I felt the emphasis on every word as if articulately reading in slow motion. The teacher looked quite proud of her attempt at humiliating me. The experience was quite the contrary.

I vividly remember the emotional intensity of reading the note out loud to my entire class. My body may have been trembling, and yet I felt exhilarated to express my feelings for him to my entire class. The excitement continued to the present as I remembered that I knew it was him all along.

Chapter 40:

Stone Tablet

I awoke with the vision of a marble sculpture holding an empty tablet. The man of my dreams urged me to write about cause and purpose. He wanted to know why I wanted to be with him and why I think we are better together. As I wrote, the information flowed as if from an eternal source of higher knowledge.

I want to be with him because of all the dreams and visions across time. He helped me in the past metaphysically by visiting me in my dreams. We are supportive of each other individually and collaboratively as friends in the present. Our values, goals, and mission are aligned. The dreams show us happy and prosperous together. Our present becomes our future, and we are strong and powerful together as a couple.

We are equals in intellect and talent. Our ambitious aspirations are aligned. Our combined intellect, intuition, and ideas bring us to a higher level together. When we combine our talents, we generate something new of high vibration that's universally applicable.

As I focused intently on determining more details, the following statements entered my consciousness: "We have the power to create something more together than either of us could create alone. This creation of love will provide hope and benefit many people in spiritual transformation."

We came together on a higher level of consciousness, and when we are together in this lifetime, we bring the higher level of consciousness into our everyday waking reality. The higher level of consciousness is expansive and invigorates our entire lives and all our experiences. We bring more to life together.

We are better together in love, sharing joy, intelligence, ideas, and insights of higher creativity. I am going to teach people how to access and read their timelines. Reading our timeline is how I developed this ability. Together, we experience the expanse of emotional and physiological activation of energetic light and euphoric, fuzzy, tingly, electric bliss.

I wanted to avoid my emotions but was briefly distracted by a song within my mind. The lyrics communicated the love shared across time. The song was an indication to write about my emotions.

As the song played, I felt light energy, a feeling of complete appreciation, contentment, admiration, and love. The feelings extended, pulsating and vibrating through my veins as a feeling of permanent progressive love and adoration. The transformative power of these feelings penetrates, deeply inspiring me. The manifestation of love permeated throughout my energy, body, mind, and emotions, and beyond the physical level of consciousness.

I feel genuine gratitude for my dreams of you that brought me to you. I appreciate having you in my life as a supportive friend. I always look forward to hearing from you and encourage you to keep contacting me. Excitement overtakes me each time I reach out to you and share my experiences with you. I want to be with you because I love you now, and I loved you in the dreams in the past, and I continue to love you in the future. We loved each other in a past life. We love each other in this life. We continue to love each other in the future. Our love occurs on all levels: spirit, mind, and body, and radiates energetically across time and space.

We are meant to fulfill our current life purpose together. The world we create together is one of virtue and unconditional love for all time, and our love takes us higher. The more vibrantly and colorfully we experience the blissful aspects of love together, the more we fulfill our life's mission. We are meant to travel far and experience various cultures and all this life offers us. This life is meant to be enjoyed and experienced to the fullest, most luxuriously, extravagantly glamorous, all in an adventurous way.

We found each other now because we are ready now. Do everything and do it now. Enjoy our physical bodies and experience physical pleasure. Enjoy the external world and the beautiful aspects of the sun, sea, sand, mountains, deserts, and lush vegetation of tropics and forests. Immerse ourselves in exotic cultures. The more we experience, the more we learn. Expand our collective consciousness, intellect, and intuition collaboratively. Unity of our parts generates wholeness as one mind, body, and spiritual energetic vibration.

We are companions in creation, travel, and the sharing of adventure. We are nurturing and supportive, viewing the world in unity for the joy of life, feeling blissful happiness, love, light, and laughter. Our outcome is joy, ecstasy, and transformative, vibrant experiences of pure potential through harmonious union beyond the dreams and into reality. All my dreams become our reality. We enjoy each other on this fun adventure, wide-awake, all in now.

The magic happens when intuition (spirit), intellect (mind), emotions, and physiological (body) are all congruently focused on the same intention. As Carl Jung stated, "To make what fate intends for me my own intention." I have reached this point of congruence with excitement to experience the magical manifestation of this love at the fullest level of wild intensity with the man of my dreams in this life, wide awake and vibrantly colorful now.

Thank You

Thank you for finding me in my dreams and guiding me to find you in this lifetime. Thank you for meeting me on a higher level. I am forever grateful for all you helped me with and guided me through on a higher level. Thank you for the guidance, dreams, warnings, protection, growth, commitment, and neutral, supportive presence.

Thank you for being a supportive friend in real life. Thank you for listening to me and being open to hearing about my dreams. Thank you for reaching out to me, calling me, texting me, and sharing your projects with me. I love being a part of your life. Thank you for welcoming me openly.

I became your favorite everything, the one you call when you have something exciting to share, the one you call because you trust me, value my support, and know I love you and am here as your friend. I feel the greatest satisfaction in knowing you felt comfortable reaching out to me when your intuition was overwhelming. I feel gratitude for my ability to help you.

I am the woman of your dreams. I show up, reciprocate, and love you in all the ways that best support you. I love you as you are and continue to love you through your growth and evolution as you reach your highest authentic potential. I am your ideal lover and partner for life. Welcome the loving sensations physically, mentally, spiritually, and energetically with compassion in a harmonious union.

Chapter 41:

Confirmation Beyond Words

I stripped my clothes off and clicked the Zoom link with the camera off for his session. He said, "You might have stripped off your clothes and be naked." I double-checked, and yes, the camera was off. At that moment, I wondered how he knew that I did, in fact, strip off my clothes to get comfortable and I was naked.

After the call, I texted him and asked if he reads us even if the camera is off. His response was basically yes, and then he asked some follow-up questions to determine exactly how well and how often he reads me.

I responded, "All the time, and sometimes, you say things that were in my head or that I had written previously. You said, 'You might be naked,' as I was lying on my bed naked for the call."

He asked, "Were you freaked out?"

"I checked that the camera was off. I am fine with you remote viewing or actually seeing me like that."

He replied, "I only see what is within my imagination."

The texts were coming in rapidly, and we were both excited. I lost track of the conversation and didn't know if his comments were about him remote viewing or actually seeing my naked body. I answered all comments congruently, knowing that the answer was the same. "Absolutely, I know I will show you. I've seen it."

I knew he was significant in my life when he continually entered my dreams. I saw our future to bring us together to fulfill our soul purpose. The memories of the future are divine consciousness, leading us in the direction we are meant to go. The dreams brought us together. Reading and telepathy bring us together. Keep showing up. We are each other's ultimate relationship.

Could he be as deeply invested in manifesting the perfection of our relationship as I am? Yes, we manifested each other. His words, being the same as I had written from the dreams, keep occurring as more confirmations.

What was his intention? His intention to find his ideal mate put him in my dreams. I became his focused intention. With my intention and desire to find him, I found him.

I remembered when we first met, and I told him about him being in my dreams. He thinks he came to me in my dreams. He told me that in person at the time and via text after. He manifested all this as much as I did. He manifested me as much as I manifested him. We were both manifesting our ideal relationship with each other simultaneously.

Soon after we met, he asked me if I was familiar with the Silva method. I had slept through the audiobook once before and was curious, so I listened to the audiobook again and fell asleep again, waking up to just one statement: "The Silva method will attract your ideal mate to you and make your ideal mate find you." Though I later discovered this statement did not exist in the book, it was the only explanation and completely accurate summary of what was happening.

As we got closer in real life, he became more persistent in the dreams. In the dreams, I know he wants deep emotional connection and to experience emotional commitment. He wants only me and wants me to commit to only him. He is fiercely loyal and protective. Loyalty is important to him. He wants reassurance and for me to openly express my feelings.

In a dream, I found myself in a situation where I chose him from a group of men who were interested in me. As I made my choice, I communicated my decision to him telepathically. I told him that I choose him now and always, under any circumstances and over all other options. My feelings for him are so intense that there is no other choice, even if it may seem so. The only choice is him. It's as if he projected himself into my dream, seeking the absolute truth of my intentions.

My dreams have always felt authentic, as the place where the genuine truth is presented beyond interference, alteration, or analytical resistance of the waking level of consciousness. And the closer we became, the more focused I was on him in both the dreams and in my waking life, surrendering to him completely, allowing the dreams to come true just as we both wanted all along.

A week later, he answered my unarticulated question and confirmed what I had perceived when he said, "Melissa, remember your metaphor about the eggs, you already know that incubation is gestation. You have incubated what you want to come into your life. All you have to do now is surrender and allow it to hatch in your life when it is ready. You can't do anything to speed it up. I know you have a lot of fire energy and all, but can't you be patient a while longer?"

He is consciously aware of my intentions. He will come to me when the time is right, and he is ready. Have patience. Give space. Accept what is given in its time. Receive. Enjoy each moment completely. Build a strong foundation for everlasting love.

Through this journey, I've come to understand that manifestation unfolds in its own time and in its own way. I've learned to be patient and trust in the process. When the time is right, our relationship will manifest perfectly as it's meant to be. I trust that nothing can prevent what's meant to happen from happening. The dreams were incubation. They revealed the highest potential and support our union on a higher level of consciousness. The ongoing relationship with my intuition inspires me to follow the exciting path and wait for the future memories, as revealed in my dreams and visions, to become reality.

Chapter 42:

Dreams Come True

I saw a beautiful sunset on the West Coast while sitting next to him, feeling his arm around me, embracing me as we enjoyed the motion of the waves and sand on our feet with gratitude for our wonderful life. Awake and in awe, the vision was so vivid that I could feel the sand on my feet and see the golden sun brightly shining into my eyes.

The sun became so bright that I watched the future memory in sepia. In the vision, we existed as black silhouettes moving around in front of me as if I were watching a nostalgic movie of us. I felt love and happiness throughout my mind, body, and emotional expression as I enjoyed our future memories.

As I reoriented to the present reality, the feeling of the sand on my feet was so intense that I took off my sandals and brushed the sand off my feet. As I shook the sand out of my sandals, I wondered where all the sand came from. I could not recall ever wearing those sandals to the beach.

The tablet dream came true on the same day. He articulated the action of chiseling in stone as he provided direction to write our intentions, why, and emotions as if they were being chiseled in stone. I was wide-awake, alert, and thoroughly amused by the fact that every dream was coming true.

Later that evening, I shared the tablet dream with him and told him that my emotions came in a song. He asked what song, and I told him "When I Look Into Your Eyes" by FireHouse without providing any context. I refrained from telling him that I wrote about my intentions for our relationship or that the song applied to my emotions for him. The Star tarot card entered my mind as I hit send on the typed message. Everything is coming to life. We are manifesting ideal love.

The following day, I realized my fitness goals were achieved as my abs had become a rock-hard sculpture of perfection. The joy and excitement of this achievement filled me with a sense of playful optimism and adventure. I confidently shared that I had met my fitness goal, knowing he is attracted and draws closer to me. He will pursue me and make a move to romance. He sees my level of loyalty and commitment. He feels my rock-hard abs are what he asked for in a partner, and without telling me or me stating that goal, together we achieved it. This is his confirmation. A passionate fire of divine feminine attraction is awakening, inspiring me to continue on this path of self-improvement and manifestation.

And then I received confirmation of my confirmation of his confirmation as he discussed creating the woman of his dreams with a detailed description. When you visualize them clearly, they come into your life. Your focus shapes your experience of reality. My dreams and waking reality have merged into one.

Chapter 43:

Shine Brightly on Stage

Suddenly, I realized he saw what I saw when I shared that I had already bought the sequin dress for that big stage event that I know will happen. He completely understood the message when I shared a song as a testament to showing up as my authentic, fiery, confident self, ready for success with intrinsic motivation for my enduring persistence over the years. The dress purchase was a symbolic act of my belief in the future I am manifesting, and I could feel his shared excitement and anticipation for this event.

Instantly, I felt a rush of excitement and fiery confidence as I listened to music and was surprised with confirmation beyond expectation when I heard a new song. The song played so fast that I couldn't catch the name, but I definitely received the message. He enjoys my fiery wild and wants to be famous and pursue my dreams with me.

He called me soon after, and his tone was upbeat and excited. I confidently told him I see myself wearing that sequin dress on a big stage as I teach people how to read their timelines psychically, a practice of accessing intuition and energy to view future events. I emphasized showing people how not just to imagine but actually psychically view their future. He shared ideas of how I could get closer to that outcome by attracting a following and offering my services now. He was supportive and encouraged the pursuit of my dreams.

Fiery confidence and vibrant, passionate enthusiasm were the energies I felt within my mind, body, and the energy around me. I received his acknowledgment of my persistent determination. In that moment, I felt fiercely loyal to and focused on striving toward my dreams. It all begins in our minds as we prepare to live our best lives. Be prepared to step into the spotlight as the center of attention.

A montage displayed a sequence of future seminars where we were on the main stage. It was a preview, an inspired vision of us as lovers joining together to celebrate our creative hypnotic skills on stage. I heard the cheers and excitement of our audience. I felt the collective excitement of our success. I saw the bright lights on stage and above, with various colors and effects to highlight us in the spotlight. I could also feel the sun's warmth and the sea's soothing effects as we traveled. I felt freedom, fun, excitement, joy, and love. The words I heard him say to me in the vision were success and satisfaction as we watched everything flow in our lives. There is epic fame with many stage performances, laughter, hugs, and fun. I see it in our smiles and feel it in our tender embrace, inspiring a sense of freedom and joy in the vision of our future success.

I saw us boldly confident and congratulatory expressing our feelings of love and support to each other on large stages with vast audiences. Our body language communicated the loving rapport, trust, and support of each other in our relationship. We appealed to the audience as if impenetrable, ecstatic in a perfect relationship, appearing illuminated as if rising above the crowd. The audience admires us and feels inspired by the words in our message. We are in an elegant, harmonious dance of love on the highest level, collaboratively raising the vibration of our audience. We are articulate, plentiful, and wealthy. We exude pure loving intentions toward each other eternally in celebration of transformative coincidences that led to the enlightenment of our union in this life. Together, we always win. Love is meant to be felt with wild intensity.

The dreams and visions are the previews leading me to keep showing up as my bold, authentic, fiery, confident self. Keep sharing. Allow the dreams to manifest into the highest potential of my best life. Let the adventure find me. Be ready. Accept and allow the unknown because it's part of the process. Keep the confirmations coming as every vision becomes our waking reality. Allow love to flourish in its own time and in its own way. Allow it to become what it is meant to be in the same way I knew a year before writing *Wild Intensity* that it would be a love story about the connection of consciousness. I knew that I would discover the meaning of connection of consciousness, and it is the spiritual bond that transcends physicality.

Chapter 44:

Success

There were many times when I wanted to see more, know more, hear more, experience more. I just wanted to know what's next, and once I knew that, I wanted to know what else. Future and past events are revealed to me out of the sequence of time. Time is perceived differently on higher planes of consciousness. I allowed our real-life story to evolve naturally as our time came into the present and as I received more glimpses of our timeline. I accepted that some elements are meant to remain a mystery until their time arrives.

A vivid memory of a long-forgotten experience surfaced as I attempted to view more of our future events. I was outside the home where I once lived fifteen years before we met. He appeared as an apparition glowing in golden light and took on a solid form as we gazed at each other. The intimacy of eye contact with this man felt angelic, and yet it was somewhat distressing to this lesser-evolved past version of myself.

The experience was new to me then, and I felt vulnerable. I felt protective of my thoughts and fearful of judgment. I felt exposed and raw, in despair at that point. I did not yet know he was a person or that he was going to be significant in my future.

In an instant, he looked through my eyes, and I looked through his eyes at me. It was more than a reflection and beyond imagination. It was a vivid memory of the first time he looked through my eyes, and I looked through his eyes in an exchange of consciousness. This was an earlier time in my life, and it was the first time we met on a higher level of consciousness that I am aware of in this lifetime. I felt the connection between us, the rapport and polarity of attraction on a higher level.

Who was he? He was blond, muscular, and tan. His eyes were blue, and suddenly, they were the same shade of green as mine. How did his eyes change colors? Do I know this man? Something about him seemed familiar. Why did he visit me here? I was unwell energetically, spiritually, and emotionally. Why did I forget about this until now? I saw myself through his eyes. A hollow ghost of myself was all I saw. I wanted to help her, but she was distant and unavailable amid a dark night of the soul.

Though I had consciously intended to visit the future and experience the exchange of consciousness in a future moment, higher levels of consciousness intervened. I was taken to the past to meet him at that pivotal time. It was quite unsettling to see myself at a diminished capacity. However, meeting myself in that place through his eyes changed my perspective about what happened in that era as the long-forgotten memory surfaced.

As I analyzed this metaphysical experience, the next level of success was revealed, and I realized how I plan to do timeline work. It is entirely possible to visit the future and past simultaneously. The future and the past meet at various places in time. All versions meet simultaneously and can evolve together, healing the timeline by accepting and making amends with the past and choosing a higher path forward.

As I contemplated the memory of this experience, I could see him standing over me as if we were in the present time, and he said the word "success." This reminded me of all that had been overcome, all the challenges and obstacles I had faced and conquered. It reminded me to look back and watch all the experiences that changed me and led me toward constant learning and evolving my mindset.

It was also a testament to continue to level up. It took many years to become ready for a significant loving relationship on a higher energetic level. The memory was to show me my success. The next time I heard him speak in real life, as always, I received confirmation of the words he said to me in the memory as he talked about the inevitability of success.

We found each other in physical form in this lifetime. Our initial contact began through the connection of consciousness on a metaphysical level. Our life together is now. I became comfortable with intense eye contact during our higher-level connection of consciousness. I look forward to the intimacy of eye contact with him in real life.

I then drifted into a sex dream and a montage of travel, beaches, and seminars with the man of my dreams in our future. Reflecting on our future experiences fills me with excitement and eagerness for what is to come.

Chapter 45:

Music as a Time Portal

Music takes us forward in time. The connection of consciousness sent songs that were just ahead of time. It was only in retrospect that the magnitude resonated with me. I was so excited as I lived the experience each day. I loved the feelings and validation I received from the music, knowing I would have precisely what I hoped for and was striving toward. The relationship would strengthen and unite to the next level, and the impact of my talent would reach a larger audience. It was as the music evolved and showed me more that I realized just how powerful the effect of music is on manifestation and revelation. I felt inspired and motivated to continue to forge ahead.

The music can also take you back to a different era in time. Choose a song from a different place in time. What is the era in time? Where are you in your life during this song? Access your past or future memories. Remember when this song first resonated with you? Where were you? Who were you with? What qualities and feelings did you experience?

Choose a favorite song or lyric. Listen to the music. What is the song? Do you hear the lyrics? What do the lyrics indicate? Bring the awareness into your mind. Imagine you step into this song and feel it completely. How do you feel as you bring that feeling into your body now? Experience the sensations of the beat, tone, tempo, and pace, moving your body. What do you feel in your physiology and your emotions?

How does this song inspire you in your life? Does it improve your attitude, enlighten your feelings, give action steps to your goals, or improve your mindset in a time of uncertainty? What are the inspirational messages? What are your action steps? Where are you going? What will you do next?

The music can accelerate your timeline. As the music takes you forward in time, where are you going? Where does the music take you? What emotions do you feel? What actions will you take? Imagine where the music takes you.

Theme Song

"Let's Love" by David Guetta and Sia repeatedly played while I lived in Florida and emphasized the dedicated companionship I aspired to for my future. The song was a source of inspiration for the relationship that I believed was on the way into my life. Initially, the song encouraged me to show up, actively participate in my life, and be open to love.

A few months before we met, while I was at the beach in the rain, the song entered my mind, thoroughly characterized my hopes, and provoked a sense of knowing he was about to enter my life. It felt as if the song was foreshadowing the wonderful times just ahead along the path. I felt a sense of emotional fulfillment throughout my body.

The song continued to frequent my mind and became a theme song, a musical embodiment of our dynamic and the depth of our connection. The song came in any time I wondered if I should reach out. My attention was drawn to nurturing the connection and maintaining supportive devotion in our relationship. The song encouraged me to show up for him and be supportive. The more we show up, the stronger our relationship becomes. What I feel, the euphoric energy and the motivation to always show up for him, is love.

Chapter 46:

Gratitude & Belief

I showed up bold with fiery confidence because I am the brightest flame. I believe that each dream shows me the path to live my best life. I chose to be in a loving, healthy, committed relationship, even as it was only in my mind for now. If I did not follow the dreams, then what was the point of all the dreams showing me the way?

The more intensely I believed in the dreams, the stronger I became in my commitment to my well-being and having the best relationship. It all began in my mind. The visions I have seen are only the beginning. Love became my focus, and I want to see the future as I have previewed in dreams come to life.

He entered my world in dreams and has been persistent in my dreams for years. We built rapport slowly. The dreams have shown our connection on a higher level. We compassionately strive for each other metaphorically and metaphysically on a higher level, encouraging spiritual growth as we prepare to be together in a peaceful, loving embrace. Our relationship was brought to us by our higher selves. We are each other's highest love and on our highest timeline together.

He invited me to his world in physical life, and I happily entered. Moving forward, it all happens suddenly, in an unexpected way that I could not foresee. The best love story of our lives awaits. We grow and thrive, rising and living in our potential. We are already in tune with each other spiritually and mentally. Next, we synchronize emotionally and physically in harmonious union in a symphony of love.

Throughout this journey, the more I allowed, accepted, believed, and listened to my intuition, the stronger and more accurate it became. The more I showed up, the more vibrantly I felt my emotions and physical sensations. I was exuberant with trust in what I saw, heard, felt, and knew as I immersed myself in the highest timeline. I achieved energetic alignment and felt life pulsating through my veins, synchronizing every cell in my body, every synapse in my brain, and every thought in my mind, living my life on the highest vibrational frequency in each moment of every day with gratitude.

Thank you for entering my dreams. Thank you for being there for me on a higher level of consciousness. You were there when I didn't even know you or know that I needed you. Thank you. I appreciate that you found me in my dreams and that you were always there. You were a constant, supportive presence for many years. You are my dream come true. I appreciate you being in my life in the present. I welcome you on all levels of consciousness. I allow, accept, and appreciate you in physical reality as you are.

Thank you for sharing your mind, body, and energetic consciousness with me on this adventure. As you openly shared your perspectives and beliefs, I felt absolute gratitude for having the honor of getting to know you as a person.

Each confirmation of my dreams brought delight and euphoric excitement for the future we will share. I continue to feel amazement at the level of detail and accuracy presented to me just in advance of our encounters.

As you talked about the nerve endings in the hands synchronizing the brain, I blissfully recalled all the visions where the touch of our hands sends all the wonderful emotional sensations throughout my body and expands our vibrant energy of light, enhancing our connection. The depth of our connection on a higher level inspires enlightenment. I appreciate the evolution of our relationship as the dreams continue to become our wakeful conscious reality.

As I wondered what else would happen next, I focused and accelerated my consciousness into the near future. He was staring into my eyes, and I intently stared back. I adored looking into his eyes, curious with desire, confidently connecting with his soul. As we stared intently into each other's eyes, a bright ray of white light emerged through us and overtook our entire bodies, engulfing us in harmonious union. The light so brightly unified us, and as the light expanded and became even brighter, I was brought back to the present moment.

I wrote, "The dreams are manifesting into our reality. The man of my dreams is my future husband, and our romantic relationship will become a physical reality soon. We exude blissful love, being at the center of attention, and feeling successful. Our energy toward each other is expansive, angelic, and magnetic."

I felt the physiological euphoric sensations throughout my body. I heard his thoughts as he said, "I can read your thoughts."

I telepathically responded, "Watch my future visions of us."

After a quiet pause that felt like days, I heard him say, "I'll come running back for more."

What happened next was beautiful and magnificent. My love was apparent and became eternally expansive as I saw myself sharing visions and dreams with Maestro in the pool. My energetic presence was ethereal as I shared, and we both appeared larger than life, illuminated in the golden sun. We stayed there for hours and talked about everything, sharing our philosophies.

Dreams came true, and visions were alive. It was the beginning of expressing the intensity of my love in the physical world. I was honest with him. We have essential life-changing decisions to make. We choose to be together in divine love and romance. We take responsibility for our actions. We are on the authentic path of our intuition. Together, we achieve massive success and manifest ideal love. We feel pride in our achievements, and others recognize our accomplishments. Teamwork, generosity, and sharing skills characterize our way to prosperity in the world. There is strength when we unite as soulmate lovers and celebrate our union.

Chapter 47:

Eavesdropping

I heard his words and his voice, "I don't know. We'll have to wait and see."

Then I felt like I was eavesdropping on a conversation that began at the pool. I heard Maestro talking to him as he said, "It's like this. She thinks she is your soulmate. Now rush along and take her before someone else does. She's vulnerable now, and someone could sweep her off her feet, and then you lose, and she is gone, all because of some fussy little girl of your youth. That's not Melissa.

"She loves you and will do anything for you. She's going to cherish you, and wouldn't your life be better with that kind of love? You will want nothing else once you experience spiritual love; she feels that for you. She told me about her dreams, higher consciousness, and astral spiritual connection. She took a chance, now bus up and carry her on. Bloody chap, you are like my son; don't let a good one get away. Hell, she's fucking fabulous, a once-in-a-universe kind of woman; you need her, you want her, you desire her, and you heard her share her passion for you. Hell, mate, she dreamt of you long before she met you. What other proof do you need?

"She is the most beautiful, dashing woman here. Look around. Everyone she meets loves her. Now, quit wasting your time and go get Melissa. You won't be disappointed. If nothing else, she will be the best fuck you have ever had in your entire life, and you can have her tonight. You only have this one life; she already told you how she feels. Trust her and trust your gut. Go get her. You have nothing to lose except your fear of being with a beautiful woman who made the move.

"You remember how shy she was at the beginning. It took a lot for her to open up and tell you, man. She wanted me to do it and was then afraid I would tell you she loved you. Then I had to hypnotize her three times to talk to you. You were at the table for one of those times last night. She loves you and doesn't want to muck it up, and if you avoid her, that's it."

Next, it was as if Maestro knew I was eavesdropping and began to interact with me telepathically as he continued to talk to him.

He said, "Melissa, I'm lying now to get him to act…." as he said to him, "She's going to fuck one of these other guys here, and since she is already emotional, she will decide to have a terrible relationship with him, and she will anchor you as that evil blond man who haunted her for many years.

"Now go over there and tell her you love her too. Ask her to leave with you and tell her you want to hear the details of those dreams that show you two together. Go on an adventure with her and let her tell you your future. Ask her to have spiritual, astral sex with you. Tell her I told you how she described it, and you haven't felt it yet, and you want her to take the lead. Let her lead and enjoy it. She is fantastic. Just love her and don't hurt her. She went out on a limb for you and will do anything for you. Now get over there and talk to her.

"Get over your fear and live a passionate life with her. She's a hypnotist; she's great; everybody loves her. Look at how magnetic and radiant she is. Stop being scared to love. It won't get worse... Melissa, see the double bind there?... "Don't you want to be the man where she is on your arm, and you have a lot of pride? Show her off. She said she likes attention. She wants everyone to look at her. She attracts people to her and is a great woman who can help you. She will draw people to you. I know you are the guru of marketing and all, but she is a brand of her own, and she did it all alone simply by trusting her gut. The story of how you two came together is marketing; now look at that infinite potential.

"See, Melissa, I sold to what he cares about. I painted the end state and created the emotion of pride and competition. There you go, success."

Jezebel joined the conversation and said to him, "As soon as you fuck her, you are gonna know. Spiritual sex is so good."

Maestro confirmed. "It's amazing, man."

Jezebel said, "Go experience some love."

Maestro spoke again. "You've been through a lot; now go find out if she is the love of your life. You've got nothing to lose except the fear you created in your imagination... Melissa, now I'm going to sing to him to get him highly emotional.

"In my imagination, if you put her mind at ease, she will love you for being sensitive to her vulnerability. You will anchor her emotional state, and she will be putty in your hands. You're golden now. Live in the present.

"Melissa, now he thinks it's his idea to console and bond with you.

"And what other woman do you have so much in common with? And she is a flaming redhead; she could be the woman of my dreams. And I'd love to have a woman who is really into me like she is about you. She didn't even know me. We just met, and she shared her dreams and feelings for you. She is the authentic woman you have been manifesting. So what if she doesn't exactly fit your imagination? She's even better than the woman you imagined."

Jezebel said to him, "I like her. She is real, and you know I don't like most people. Got to give it to her; she took a risk on your friendship, and she let you know where she stands. She put it on the table, and she did it right away. Not a wallflower drooling in the corner. She is a force. She made her way into our inner circle, and you know that doesn't come easy. She belongs in our tribe. You two will be cute together. She's hot and confident, sexy just like you, and that girl's got class, and she's honest. Man, get in it with her. You know, tonight. What do you have to lose? I'll talk to her if you want and see how she is feeling. You know, as soon as you fuck her, you are gonna know."

Just briefly, I heard him say to me, "Well, you opened the loop; I'll give you that. I don't know where we go from here, and I think I want to give us a chance; I mean, why not? Your dreams brought you to me for a reason, and I hypnotized you to keep showing up."

Chapter 48:

Presque Vu

The pool acts as a strange portal for me. The water brings my wild to the surface. Bold, vibrant, outrageous confidence prevails as my dominant trait, and the siren in me exudes in her magnificent beauty and prowess. In the pool, with pure excitement, I told him my dreams show us together. I knew this was the proper next step even though he said, "I don't know how I feel about that."

It was a 5,000-year-old wizard who introduced me to the concept of Presque vu in the hours after I excitedly told the man of my dreams about our future. Presque vu explained my feelings and provoked a desire for evolution as I was on the boundary of resolution. As the days progressed, he distanced himself from me and, at times, appeared to be afraid of me. It was as if my siren vibe equally scared and intrigued him.

The reality was just like the original nightmares, where he kept appearing everywhere I was and just stared at me with the same intensity as in my original nightmares. There was a ridiculous number of men interested in me, and he was in the background, just like he was in my nightmares, watching me as I rejected each of them. He watched me from a distance as all my nightmares came true.

The dreams that felt like they were to occur in some distant timeline rapidly came true. We both wore the exact clothing I saw us wearing together on stage in the future. We even danced, something I could not imagine coming true so soon. Like in dreams, my eyes changed from green to blue and returned to green.

A symphony of lyrical intuition came through in a series of statements. "He's all about the money, money, money, and this is not the time." I am encouraged to "keep dreaming and feeling the love inside." My dad came through with a message at the end. He laughingly said, "I am proud you are a Vegas star. You are as confident as I was and as bold and blunt as I was but without the booze." As I looked at the blond man lovingly, my dad smiled and said, "Keep going. He's the one. Keep showing up and rise."

I could see every version of each dream as if I were watching multiple versions of us interacting, and I knew all my dreams would come true. My dreams accurately depict our future. We are just before our time.

Chapter 49:

Detour

A detour presents a choice to leave the beaten path and take a unique route to our destination. It's a departure from the paved highway of a continuous routine pattern or repetitive cycle. A detour provides an adventure into the unknown along the way to our destination. I parked my car and ventured onto a detour, onto the sand dunes and mounds of grasses, a landscape too rugged for vehicles. There was no map due to the shifting sands. A solo footpath was the option I had chosen.

The scenery was enticing with the sun reflecting on an ocean beyond the dunes. The sky was beautiful. Walking and exploring alone was peaceful; a feeling of serenity overtook me. After a period of exploration, I departed the wilderness and continued along with an enlightened, warm, uplifting feeling of calm. I knew where I intended to go and thoroughly enjoyed the scenic route as I had created my own detour.

As I walked along, I approached a dangerous stop along the highway where those with dark intentions met. The detour merged with the highway at this intersection, disguised as a temporary place to rest and replenish. I watched through the window as a scene reminiscent of the past emerged. I watched myself navigate as two ogre-like people attempted to block my way. I heard myself conducting self-hypnosis and narrating the scene from a higher level as the version of me in the scene took strategic action and got past the ogres untouched. I felt a sense of empowerment as all levels of my consciousness were protecting me and working together to learn lessons and thrive.

Feeling satisfied, I chose to walk further along to a coffee shop where I might wait for a ride. The duration of the wait and the amount of time it would take to walk to the coffee shop were unknown. Waiting at the coffee shop was tentative, as continuing to walk was a possibility.

Detours lead into the unknown, a realm of uncertainty and intrigue with endless options to change course. Actions may alter the course of the detour, making it longer with points of intrigue or shorter with obstacles. It's entirely possible to be unaware of the details that were always going to occur along the way. Just like those blind spots generated by mountains and curves when you look from above at a scenic overlook. You can't always see what's ahead.

Sometimes, he differed from the person he was in my dreams. It was difficult for me to see him as he was when I knew and deeply loved a dream version of him. I could see that he was off the path of the person he was in my dreams. It was apparent to me that he was off his authentic path. He asked me to tell him if he ever differed from the person he was in my dreams, and he asked me to tell him if he was ever off the path. As I told him what I saw, the impact was dramatic. My words were not well articulated or well-received, and there was no turning back.

Even though I seized the moment, confident in my chosen path, I began to question everything. I wondered why my dreams brought me to him. Why did I feel compelled to keep showing up? Did he really hypnotize me to keep showing up? What were his true intentions?

The final statement entered my mind as a lyric to a song that does not even exist: "Love will come, and love won't fall away." Love is a constant force, regardless of the changes and challenges we face. Love is present on whatever path is chosen as long as it leads to the destination. Move forward wherever the road may lead and accept the unexpected detours. After all, it is interesting when unexpected things happen, and the unexpected keeps life interesting.

And I wonder, are we ever really off the path? Perhaps we just chose to go the long way. The detour just might be along the scenic route, and we are always on the way to our destination. And I wonder, does a detour even exist, or was it always the way?

Chapter 50:

The Pinnacle

I felt discouraged along the detour until I remembered that a step back is a part of the dance. The past informs the present and influences our choices. I thought about my college era and the times I spent with The Pinnacle. He is the man who set the standard for intellect, emotional stability, maturity, and sexual compatibility requirements for all future relationships. Were they intelligent, loyal, compassionate, respectful, and stable? Would they accept me as I am without judgment? Could they accept my wild without attempting to tame me? Was I too much for them?

I vividly remember my first date with The Pinnacle. We went to the club district downtown. I was wearing my shiny royal blue silicone pants as he confidently bit my ass at the table in front of our friends. We were hot from there. That look of love, attraction, and adoration began on our first date. I remember that look in his eyes each time we reconnected in person after every gap in time, no matter how long or short, even if it was just a day. I remember when we saw each other in the classroom building, and he had that look, and I was so excited that I dropped all my papers.

The Pinnacle's alias was given as he once told me I was his pinnacle. How did I become his pinnacle? Sexually, we were completely open and wildly in sync: sensual, supportive, experimental, and expressive with each other. The Pinnacle is a testament to longevity and endurance.

Our friendship withstood the test of time over twenty years and all of life's circumstances. Whenever time lapses, we pick up where we left off as if no time has elapsed. The Pinnacle was a source of stability during chaos. Complete openness and trust in each other without judgment or condemnation characterized our dynamic. A core value was derived from our intellectually stimulating conversations and the respectful acceptance of each other in each facet of our lives.

Whenever a significant event was on the horizon, The Pinnacle magically became present in my life as if he was a marker in the universe as I chart the way. I wondered if he had reached out because it's about to get real with the man of my dreams.

The Pinnacle was a source of stability and strength, a buoy in the sea, always somewhere in the distance, a marker along the way. Always there, firmly anchored as a marker of a place in time from a long time ago, a place of long-term friendship visiting each other's worlds from afar. The Pinnacle, a man with brown hair and brown eyes, is not the destination because that relationship was already all it would be in its time. We navigated the way together many years ago, but our paths diverged. The sea took us in different directions.

I appreciate life's experiences that brought me to this time in my life as it is now. A reflector mirrors back all that I have seen, and there is safety as I continue along my way. Showing what's behind, dangers to avoid, a marker on the path, a memory, a foundation of formation, guiding the safest path to keep going. A reminder of where I most want to go as I keep moving along with the sea. Find that blond man in the sea. Live your best life with him.

All our past experiences influence how we navigate the present. As I temporarily edited out the sensual components, I kept hearing and seeing words that I must keep the sensual components. The sensual components add thrill and eroticism to life. An emoji communicating the perspective of The Pinnacle inspired me to go even deeper into the sensual components of the story. I thought about our relationship over twenty years ago and how those early erotic romantic experiences influenced who I am today. The longevity, endurance, and depth of our relationship over the years set the standard for what I expect of my relationships.

And, he confirmed that I remain his pinnacle.

Chapter 51:

Surrender

The Ace of Pentacles, a symbol of prosperity and abundance, appeared in my dreams and continued to appear in each deck I drew from before, during, and after Las Vegas. When I wandered solo by the souvenir shop, the Zultar machine called me over, and the Ace of Pentacles was within the display. This symbolizes the beginning of my journey toward prosperity and abundance in the real world. I am committed to investing in myself, taking action, and believing in my success. I have all the necessary resources to succeed and will succeed at anything I intend.

Above all else, I trust my intuition and higher wisdom. I value spiritual guidance for harmony and positive energy to encourage unity. I can achieve this great mission through persuasion, love, and compassion. Focus on bringing people together. I radiate loyalty, protection, and guidance. As I confidently explore the unknown and take more significant risks for growth in all aspects of my life, I am excited about the new beginnings and boundless potential that will arise.

The man of my dreams returns to be a part of the power couple I see us becoming when I am more popular and well-known. This is the beginning of prosperity and abundance, where we join and travel the world. And then, I suddenly grasped the true essence of surrender. It's not about giving up. Surrender is letting go of my agenda and allowing him to come to me in his own way and in his own time. The epiphany completely disrupted my pattern, and I let go.

While I distanced myself from him in my waking life, there were intense dreams where he sought my attention. The dreams became physically invasive. I was awoken by his physical contact with me in the dreams. I felt the physical contact as if he was actually there touching me. I felt as if his hand was within mine, like when we danced, and it startled me awake.

In another sequence, the blond man took the middle seat beside me on a plane. I wanted to touch him and rest my head on him, but I didn't know if he wanted that. All I knew was that he cared what the people behind us thought. I offered him gum, and he wanted the gum inside my mouth. We exchanged a shy, gentle, wet kiss. The sensation of the wet kiss slightly awoke me as if we had just kissed.

And I went back to sleep, observing that he cared if people saw us together. Another version of the blond man was behind us, watching me interact with him. This version of him wanted me to wait and have the experience with him on his terms when he is ready.

As I awoke, the lyrics of a vaguely familiar song played slowly in my mind to grasp the meaning of the words. He saw me shine brightly as I presented and interacted with the community. He hadn't thought of me in that light as I used to watch him perform. He now sees me as attractive, boldly confident, and standing out in my appearance. He noticed how many men wanted to be near me. He was taken aback when I told him how I felt. He was where he wanted to be when he danced with me. I could hear, see, and feel the words "I love you."

The music felt inspirational, though perhaps aspirational. The current reality did not match the dreams or the songs. I chose to redirect my focus off the dreams and songs and empowered my playlist by selecting songs of feminine strength to proceed solo. I acknowledged that I was too much for him. Even as I altered my playlist, songs invaded my thoughts, reminding me he was the man of my dreams from many years ago and would continue to be. Tarot cards continuously indicated that we would manifest the dream of ideal love and travel the world together as bold leaders.

My intuition came in even more rapidly as I redirected my focus. The concept of time was altered. It was too fast to document and too slow to forget. I received warnings of relatives' challenges immediately before they called to reveal the challenges. I heard words before they were spoken. I saw sequences of events before they happened. Verifiable proof came as an angel appeared in a reflection I took a picture of. I described a story about a jellyfish before a jellyfish appeared in a show precisely as I had described. It was all a series of confirmations showing me to trust my intuition, and it was exciting.

Creative awareness reveals wild intensity and becomes wild illumination as time advances and merges with present reality. I happily enjoyed the fantasy version of him, knowing I would continue to dream of him. The fantasy will evolve into the reality I have foreseen in my dreams. My dreams always come true.

Late one night, I awoke to write unfamiliar words. "Anoint for goodness shall behold upon us a love for eternity. Shelter and protection. Surrender conjecture. Boldly communicate. Openly reveal love's true intentions. Allow us to manifest. Expectantly await. Divine intervention brings us together."

Union

Once I really let go of the man of my dreams, shredded all my notes, and decided not to write anymore, he entered a dream. I could see him standing in the distance. His expression was one of happiness and contentment. The sky was dark as he stood by a large piece of farm equipment in front of a tire much taller than him. He motioned for me to approach him. It was as if I was floating from above and viewing from various perspectives while I walked toward him. I asked him what he was doing. He said he was waiting. The union felt predestined and orchestrated from a higher level, as if others were watching this fateful union in motion. The timing felt as if the union was a long time coming and as if no time had elapsed at all. As I approached, I felt confident joining him and equally confident in waking up and continuing my life without him.

Chapter 52:

Angels & Milk

While attempting to disregard my intuition, the signs became blatant and impossible to ignore. A reflection of an angel appeared on the ceiling in my office, and the only cloud in the sky appeared as an angel above the pool. Another angel appeared in the Northern Lights and more reflections followed. I photographed and shared the images and received confirmation from friends. The physical proof was evident.

When I questioned the interpretation and validity of the sights, dreams once again became physically invasive and rapidly came true. I dreamt of pumping breast milk into glasses and awoke to my breast lactating. As the day progressed, signs and messages were everywhere in the trees, succulents, and within. All power and sustainability exist within.

From the deciduous trees, I felt a sense of being prepared for a harsh winter with all the nutrients stored within and ready to blossom when conditions become optimal. From a succulent growing in salty sand in seemingly impossible conditions, I felt a sense of the nourishment stored in the roots and moisture stored in the leaves and a feeling of stability in the wind as if the changing winds would provide. My breasts, the trees, and the succulents were strong, stable, and prepared for whatever comes next. Each may remain dormant, awaiting optimal conditions, and when the conditions are optimal, the milk flows, providing nourishment, the tree blossoms, and the succulents grow. Wild wisdom is instinctual and generates from within, providing its essence at the appropriate time.

The following day, I was approached and asked if a storage room could be utilized for breast pumping. I was astonished as yet another of the most peculiar dreams had come true. This time, my empathic abilities took on a physical manifestation. I felt as though I had become a bit too sensitive and overly tuned into my skills. Yet, it was inspirational, and I felt a sense of empowerment from my abilities. It was once again time to redirect my focus to show myself how my dreams became a reality.

I determined with absolute certainty that I am highly sensitive, and my daily surroundings and the people I am around directly impact me. I didn't need any more proof to believe that my intuition has shown me what I know is going to happen regardless of any present circumstances and regardless of anyone's assessment, judgment, disbelief, or critique of me. The concepts of déjà rêvé (already dreamed) and déjà vu (already seen) didn't quite explain my experiences. Even though I could not find a scientific explanation, I had complete confidence in my precognitive abilities. I had always documented the dreams before they became a reality, thus generating facts rather than feelings, which created validity in my mind.

I believed my knowledge in advance had no effect on the outcome, even when I shared what I know and am. Though, there were times when I wondered if I shared too much or not enough. The concept of time was altered whenever I shared, and more dreams came after sharing. I had a series of intense dreams after I shared the lactation dream and real-life manifestation with the man of my dreams.

Reminiscent of the original dreams, it was as if the blond man were watching my memories with me, but now he was taking the lead and entering dramatic, intimate, and exciting events that are going to happen in our future. After reflecting upon my memories of The Pinnacle, I dreamt of the blond man biting my ass in public while I was wearing shiny dark-purple vegan leather leggings. It was clear to me that he wanted me. The sensation was so intense that I was awoken. In this sleep-wake state, I realized he wanted me to be powerful and prestigious. While shopping for Halloween the next day, I found those leggings at Gabe's for $2 and could not resist purchasing them.

Next, I was within a memory and a dream of the intimate details of the sexual experiences from the relationship the man of my dreams wanted me to end in those nightmares years ago. Suddenly, within the dream, he entered that man's body and enjoyed the sensual pleasure of my skills. And I remember that very experience as that man told me he was enjoying that so much that he felt as if he zoned out and didn't remember all of it. I now know it was because the man of my dreams had overtaken him and had the experience with me.

In yet another dream of a sensual memory, he was there to take me beyond that relationship to have the experiences with him that I had rejected in that relationship. I felt as if he knew I was saving those experiences for the reciprocal loving relationship I knew was my final relationship and destiny.

Throughout this journey, I have felt complete confidence in knowing that our union is inevitable.

Chapter 53:

Discover What's Next

I like to know what's next. If I know what's next, I won't miss opportunities. Previewing the future allows me to prepare for the life coming to me and the best days ahead. I often feel like I'm eavesdropping on my future and have come to enjoy it. The future that my intuition has shown is so much more vibrant than I could have ever imagined. The time of my life awaits.

If you know what will happen next, you can make better choices now. An easy way to access your intuition is by entering a state of creative awareness: alert, calm, open, and perceptive while going about your day. This state generates alpha brainwaves, allowing you to use your mind more dynamically and efficiently by working with your brain's natural rhythms. When you are relaxed and focused, you have enhanced receptivity and increased perception. When you are in a state of creative awareness, think about what you want to know or ask, "What's next?" This question may take you to any point in the future.

Future emotional highlights are accessible in this way. Allow your intuition to flow and accept it as it comes. You may discover the most effective path to get what you desire or find that what is coming is even better than what you imagine you want.

Once you set the intention to see further ahead in the timeline, the information will come. What's next may be revealed in various ways, such as in dreams, songs, writing, pictures, reading, metaphors, and visualizations. The information may all connect to show you the story. Awareness and expectation provide the format to make the connection. You may have a vision or dream followed by a song or an image of something that confirms what you see. All the repetitions that display the same message confirm what you asked for. The more you pay attention and trust the information, the more it will come. Allow, accept, and appreciate it with love.

How do you know? You know by the way it feels. How do you notice what is a message? Pay attention to combined messages when you discover similar stimuli. These are repetitions that are separate from algorithms. For example, a dream and a song showing the same signs during the day or dreaming of a place and then unexpectedly finding that place. Imagine having a dream about the Northern Lights and then seeing a bumper sticker of the Northern Lights or looking up how to call in a pigeon, and the next day a tame pigeon arrives without calling it in.

Be playful as you discover what is next for you. It's fun to play with intuition, anticipate what's next, and enjoy the mystery as it unfolds. When you see what is next and like what you see, keep that image present in your mind; you may revisit it to access more details. As you approach that place in time, you will discover imminent clues. Access your intuition to live your best life. Discover the wonderful upcoming events and collaborate with your intuition to create the best version of your story. Intuition guides you to experience the best moments of your life, and accessing your timeline provides hope, a preview, and preparation for what's to come.

Knowing what is next allows your mind the opportunity to prepare. You may discover something so amazing that you can't even believe it to be possible for you. You may experience fear or resistance, even of the good things to come. This may occur when the ego mind isn't quite ready. There may be some spiritual or emotional growth to fulfill first. When you feel resistance, write it down to capture it before it fades away. Intuition can be subtle or fleeting when you begin to work with it, so writing it down is a way to record the information as it is revealed. Then, look at it later when your mind is more receptive to processing the information. Looking back, it will be clear: an "Aha, I knew it!"

Chapter 54:

Access Your Timeline

Keep your mind open and invite your consciousness to reveal your future. Ask: What's next? Or ask a specific question to focus on an aspect of your future that you want to preview. Be receptive to the possibility of seeing beyond your current awareness. Visualization gives you a preview, which builds a sense of confidence about your future.

Visualize any future point or any place in your life. Watch that scene unfold. What do you see? What are you doing? View yourself from various perspectives. How do you feel? Feel it now in your body. Feel any physiologic emotion in your body. Step into your body. What do you feel as your future self? How do you respond and act in that place? What are the details that bring you here to this future? What inspires you about this future?

You may realize and now know what you want most in your life. What is it? See it in vivid detail. Imagine you are living your best life in this vision. Bring that feeling in your physical and emotional senses to the here and now with a complete memory of your future, knowing it will happen at its best time. Accept it. Allow it as you excitedly welcome your new life, knowing what's next. If you place your intention there, it will happen!

Chapter 55:

Illuminate with Intensity

Be an active participant in your life. Ask yourself: What do I want for my life? Search for the highest potential. Raise your vibration. Create an authentic, vibrant life. Express the brutally honest truth to yourself with integrity and courage. This is where your power grows. Set aspirations. Be specific, definite, and exact. Generate the details of the narrative. Write about it, take photos, and discover the songs that support it. Add lyrics to inspire what you desire. Gain a visual in your mind for reference. Feel the sensations and emotions of living that lifestyle.

Give it a story, a life, a plan, and a way for your intuition to guide you to the path. Find the way to your visual paradise. When you are clear and confident in your desire, the space is created for that to appear in your life.

Access your intuition to reveal even higher aspirations beyond your current awareness or imagination. Ask to see what's next. Ask your dreams and get to know the people in that place.

Believe in your dreams. Believe in yourself. Believe what you see and feel, and know it will become your reality. Confirmation is inspiration. Your intuition will guide you to attract your highest potential with magnetism. Be ready. Be confident and know that the proper steps will appear at the moment. Take the steps forward as they present.

Your intuition is available as your partner to create the life you desire. You will have what was revealed to you by your intuition, and when you follow the guidance of your intuition, you have a partner that will last a lifetime.

About the Author

Melissa Wild is the author of *Wild Intuition: An Adventure in Creative Awareness,* which readers have raved about. Melissa is a certified master hypnotist with a master's degree in creativity and change leadership. She loves swimming and nature hikes and does both to extreme—friends say she hikes like a mountain goat; they can't keep up with her.

Destination unknown, but find out more about Melissa at www.melissawildinsight.com

Bibliography of Songs:
(In order of appearance)

Taio Cruz. (2010). "Dynamite." *Rokstarr*. Universal Island Records Ltd.

The Notorious B.I.G. (1997). "Hypnotize." *Life After Death*. Bad Boy Entertainment.

David Guetta and Sia. (2020). "Let's Love." *Let's Love*. Parlophone.

NYSNC. (2000). "This I Promise You." *This I Promise You*. Jive.

The Calling. (2002). "Wherever You Will Go." *Wherever You Will Go*. RCA.

Lifehouse. (2005). "You And Me." *Lifehouse*. Geffen Records.

Extreme. (1990). "More Than Words." *More Than Words*. A&M Records.

K-Ci & JoJo. (2006). "All My Life." *The Best of K-Ci & JoJo*. Geffen Records.

Bruno Mars. (2010). "Just the Way You Are." *Doo-Wops and Hooligans*. Elektra.

Train. (2009). "Marry Me." *Save Me, San Francisco*. Columbia.

FireHouse. (1992). "When I Look Into Your Eyes." *When I Look Into Your Eyes*. Epic.

Vitamin C. (1999). "Graduation (Friends Forever)." *Graduation (Friends Forever)*. Elektra.

Bryan Adams. (1984). "Run To You." *Run To You*. A&M Records.

Bruno Mars. (2010). "Marry You." *Doo-Wops and Hooligans*. Elektra.

Disturbed. (2024). "The Sound of Silence (Cyril Remix)." *The Sound of Silence*. Reprise Records.